HIS KISSING PENALTY

A MCKNIGHT FAMILY ROMANCE

ANNE-MARIE MEYER

LUCY MCCONNELL

ORCHARD VIEW PUBLISHING LLC

1

LOTTIE

"You know what, Katie?" I swiped a piece of hair off my face and then tucked it behind my ear. "Dusting is not fun."

"No fwun," Katie repeated. The adorable little munchkin added extra sounds to her words, like language wasn't exciting enough without them. Watching my niece while I sent out resumes and did light housework for my parents hadn't been my goal upon graduation, but sometimes you just have to roll with life.

I wasn't too upset about having some time with Katie, though. I'd missed her while at school. What I did have a problem with, was being the only one of my siblings unemployed and without prospects.

Seriously, I had some major overachievers to live up to. Case in point, we were throwing a party for my older brother who had just graduated med school. The guy was a doctor, for Pete's sake—he'd had two graduation parties already. On top of that, he already worked at the local hospital...and I was cleaning my parents' house.

I had high hopes, though. One day, I'd prove I had the McKnight drive to succeed thrumming through my veins.

Today? I was a tickle monster.

I shook the dust rag at Katie and growled. She squealed and ran from the room as if a puppy nipped at her heels. The game was on. I laughed and chased after her, ready to tickle and play instead of dust. My parents never passed on a chance to throw a party. Entertaining was their life. The house was always open to friends and extended family. If any group of people lived the more-the-merrier philosophy, it was the McKnights.

And when it came to their kids, my parents were even more inviting. I knew it was a little cliché, but Mom had been begging for more of her kids to come home. So when I couldn't seem to land a job in New York—the state that *literally* held all the jobs—I told her I was moving in.

I think my hearing was still damaged from the squeal that Mom let out when I walked into the family mansion two months ago. Daddy gave me a "Welcome home, kiddo" complete with his one-armed hug and cursory pat on the back. Penelope, my older sister, was smiling as she proclaimed me her nanny. "Until you get your feet under you." Which I was okay with. I mean, Katie was adorable. And sweet. And way more fun than any stuffy businessmen I would have been working with had I taken an office job at Dad's commercial construction company.

Katie disappeared around the corner leading into the family room, her skirt kicking up behind her and her squeals filling the otherwise empty house. Just as I was about to grab her, the doorbell rang. I swung wide, brushing my fingertips over her back. She danced out of reach, and I shook my finger at her. "You've been saved by the bell, little one."

Katie skipped around the couch. "I get the dwoor."

"No, I get the dwoor." I raced her to the front entryway, pulling back at the last second to let Katie win.

She grunted as she tugged and tugged on the iron handle. Finally I reached over the top of her and pushed down the latch. The sun streamed through the open door and into the foyer, making me squint. It took a few seconds for my eyes to adjust, and when they did, I about swallowed my tongue.

Standing on our doorstep in all his six-foot-three glory, was none other than the handsome and way-too-sexy-for-his-own-good Jaxson Jagger.

My pulse did a double take and then took off at a sprint. I didn't know he was coming here, and the surprise knocked rational thought out of my head. A warning would have been nice—from anyone! Not that there was enough positive mental focus or meditation to ever prepare me to see him again; not after what had happened between us.

Jaxson's jeans hung on his hips, and he wore a pair of aviator sunglasses that gave him that bad-boy look. I tried not to roll my eyes. I knew Jaxson Jagger, quarterback. He wasn't the suave guy that he allowed women or the press to think he was. He was a softy, even if he wanted people to believe otherwise.

But I still winced as I glanced down at my cleaning clothes—a pair of skinny jeans and an oversized Wolves football tee shirt I'd stolen from my brother three years ago. I had a hole in the knee of my left pant leg, and my hair was up in a topknot and wrapped in a blue bandana. Too late, I realized I should have put on mascara this morning. But who wears mascara to tend their niece and clean house?

"Hey." Jaxson pulled off his sunglasses, revealing his emerald-green eyes. The effect was like revealing a feast to a pauper, and I stupidly drank in the sight. Apparently, I'd forgotten to take my come-down-to-earth pills this morning. Ogling Jaxson was one of the dumber things I allowed myself to do. He was practically my brother. And since my actual brother, Liam, was his best friend, I was off-limits. It was the same with any of Liam's football bros.

But as a woman, I knew a good-looking guy when I saw one. And Jaxson was good looking. His dirty blonde hair was lighter at the tips from hours in the sun. Though his fans thought he spent time in the salon, I knew better. He'd had those tips when he played high school football and lived across the hall for six months. Not that he'd ever noticed his best friend's little sister during that time of his life. I was quiet back then, even in my own home, and awed by his looks. Oh yeah, I'd noticed him and those rock-hard abs. And then there was that kiss…

I shoved the thought out of my head even as my cheeks warmed with embarrassment. Eight years had passed, and the first thing I thought of when I saw him was simultaneously the best and the worst moment of my life. No kiss since then even compared, but that didn't mean I thought about it every day. Which I didn't. I was down to once or twice a week—and that was without therapy.

Why couldn't I leave it in the past? It was a kiss. A stolen moment in time. It wasn't like my existence had started then. Although, his lips had awakened a part of me I hadn't known existed. Still. It was just a kiss. And, if he hadn't… Nope! Not going to go there.

Jaxson tucked his sunglasses into the neck of his way-too-tight tee. *Leave a little something to the imagination.* On second thought—my eyes roamed over his tight abs and the new muscles along his chest, shoulders, and arms—maybe not. *You go right ahead and broadcast your gym time all you want, big guy.* I could use a little more eye candy in my life. The guys I'd dated lately were not quite so…defined. I'd forgotten how much I enjoyed the sculpted physique. Of course, Jaxson had one of the best bodies in football. He'd won Hot Bod in *Football Inc. Magazine* two years in a row—not that I'd voted for him or anything.

"I'm here for the McKnight party." He glanced at his phone.

The party? I exchanged a look with Katie, who snuggled up to my leg. The party wasn't due to start for six hours. The staff wouldn't arrive for another three. We were not ready to entertain, and I really wanted to shower before letting guests inside. He could go to his hotel and chill for a while. "You're a little early."

"I was hoping you'd have my room ready." He picked up a duffle bag at his feet and gave me an expectant look.

"Your room?" My voice went up three octaves. It had been bad enough living across the hall from Evergreen Hollow High's most eligible football player when I had braces and bed head. I wasn't sure I could handle it now. Now that we were adults and I was…legal. Though the braces had done their job and I had decent skills with a flat iron, Jaxson had an effect on me. It was like his cologne turned my brain to mush, and I had the uncontrollable urge to giggle.

"Nantie?" asked Katie in a soft voice. She's added an "N" to auntie ages ago, and I couldn't bring myself to correct her. I'd be Nantie until she had a kid of her own. I picked her up and held her close while giving Jaxson a questioning look.

He wasted no time filling me in. "I'll be staying in the guest bedroom for a while. I'm sure Mrs. McKnight told you I was coming."

Since when did he call Mom, Mrs. McKnight? She was Brenda to everyone she'd ever fed, and she'd spent a lot of time beefing up this beefcake. But maybe he felt that, now he was an adult, he needed to be more formal, or something. So sure, I'd play along with it. "She didn't mention it."

"I can wait in the family room while you change sheets or whatever." He pushed past me and marched right in, leaving a trail of his spicy scent for me to follow. I breathed through my mouth in an effort to keep my wits about me. I could not spend my afternoon entertaining Jaxson.

Irked that he'd missed my not-so-subtle signals to stay outside, I went after him. He stopped at the stone covered archway that separated the family room from the entry and looked around. His eyes glazed over, like he was reliving a host of fond memories.

"Listen, I'm a little busy at the moment." I hitched Katie up on my hip to emphasize my point.

"Oh!" His eyes widened. "Is this Katie?" He reached for her, and she turned her face into my neck.

You go girl. Don't fall for those dreamy green eyes or his strong jaw line—this guy's a heartbreaker. My niece had better judgement when it came to men than I did. My eyes dropped once again to his chest and traced over his shoulders.

"Liam's got pictures of her all over his phone. She's his princess."

I melted a little to hear that my older brother bragged about our niece. Penny normally worked nights at the hospital, but she'd taken a few day shifts at my insistence. Being a single mother was hard enough on a regular sleep cycle, and working nights as a nurse was hard on her. But the McKnight family loved the munchkin so much that we were happy to help out however needed. Katie never lacked for love or attention even if her father's identity remained a mystery.

"She's the resident princess around here." I hitched her up again. "Can you say hi to Jaxson?"

"You know my name." He nodded his head like he'd just scored a woman's phone number.

I rolled my eyes and pointed at my tee shirt. Hello? Did he think I didn't follow my brother's team?

"You're a fan?"

"The biggest." Even when my brother Liam was Mr. Popular in high school and could have easily overlooked his shy little sister, he made time for me. We'd grown up close, only eighteen months apart and one year in school. But where Liam was bold and loud and brassy, I was shy, quiet, and, as my mom would put it, tender hearted.

"You're in for a real treat, then."

"I am?"

"Yeah, it's not just me coming back for the off-season, Liam McKnight will be here, too. He got hung up in town, so I came ahead. But he should be here soon. Then you'll get to know two of the guys on the team."

I pulled my eyebrows together. He talked as if I wasn't part of the family. As if I hadn't seen Liam shave off his eyebrow on a dare or break his arm trying to jump the fence on his ten-speed.

Holy crap! He doesn't recognize me.

My face burned. A man should recognize a girl he once kissed. Especially when it was the girl's first kiss. "Who do you *think* I am?" I managed a steady voice even though I seethed inside.

He smiled, gently tugging on one of Katie's curls. "The nanny. And I can tell you're excellent at your job, she obviously loves you."

Katie sat up and patted my cheeks. "Nantie."

Oh.

My niece's creativity with the English language may have confused him. Still, I didn't look that different, and I certainly had the McKnight heart-shaped face and my mother's smile.

My heart plummeted, and I was suddenly the invisible sixteen-year-old with a massive crush on my older brother's best friend. He hadn't seen me back then, and he didn't see me now. I may not be a doctor like Carter, or a professional athlete like Liam, or a sheriff like Mason, but that didn't mean I wasn't amazing in my own right. If people could just see past my hugely successful siblings…

I gritted my teeth. All my life I'd been the baby of the family, the caboose, the one they protected and treated like a kid. Well, I wasn't a kid anymore. I was a twenty-four-year-old college graduate who didn't have to stand here and be overlooked—again.

"Come with me." I turned on my heel and marched up the stairs. Jaxson's heavy footfalls sounded behind me.

My hair flopped in my face, and I shoved it back behind my ear with a grunt. No one walked into my house and treated me like the hired help. At the top of the stairs, I made my way down the long hallway and stopped at the linen closet at the end. "Sheets, blankets, and pillowcases are in here. I'm sure you're aware that in the McKnight house we value independence. You want a bed made, you make it yourself."

"Be sure to post a before and after picture on your Insta. I'm sure your female fans will just die when they find out you do housework too." I fanned my face dramatically.

He scowled. "Did I say something wrong, miss?"

"You said everything wrong." I glared before tromping back down the stairs. "Katie, I need a cookie."

"Yay! Cookie-num-nums." Katie wiggled down from my hip and raced to the kitchen. I didn't chase after her this time. I was too busy working out a plan. I had a little red dress hanging in my closet—one I hadn't dared pull out yet. Tonight was the night that dress was going to make its debut. Tonight, I'd be unforgettable.

I couldn't wait to see Jaxson Jagger's face when he realized his mistake.

2

JAXSON

$\mathcal{I}$ stood in my old bedroom, staring around at the faded posters and football trophies I'd won back in high school. It was strange, the sudden tug of emotions that had risen up inside of my chest at the sight of my senior year in front of me. Like a person's life could be defined by memorabilia that was now covered in dust.

Sighing, I glanced around. Coming back to this place felt like trying on a pair of football pads I'd worn as a teenager—I wasn't going to fit them the same way, or *they* weren't going to fit me. I wasn't sure which it was. Case in point, the nanny treated me like an unannounced and unwelcome house guest. I'd lived here, slept in this very bed almost my entire senior year. I thought I was more than a guest, but that cute little nanny was not impressed—not even with my team. What was up with that?

I scrubbed my face, trying to put the nanny's big, beautiful eyes out of my head. If she didn't want anything to do with me, all the better. I picked up the ancient family picture sitting on the nightstand, the one my mom had given me before they moved away and left me here. I was scrawny next to my dad.

So much had happened in the seven years since my parents were transferred to Germany. Which meant seven years since I'd even seen them. Dad, a colonel in the Marines, didn't think too highly of NFL players. To Dad, sacrifice for country meant honor—a trait he didn't feel I possessed. Not when I was the only one of my siblings to take a non-military path. It made me the black sheep of the family. The fact that I held the title of MVP going on three years now didn't matter. I wasn't good enough.

And now, I was being an idiot. Who stands in a room that looked like it hadn't been touched for years, feeling sorry for themselves? Especially when that person has everything that I had. Fame. Fortune. Women.

Sure, I didn't have a particular woman right now, but I could if I wanted to. If the stupid "one and only" that everyone claimed was out there would just show up already.

Frustrated with my lack of ability to do anything but overthink things. I grabbed my duffle and dropped it on top of the bed.

I was ready to shower this trip off and put on some clean clothes. The man I'd sat next to on the plane had been sweaty and had spent half the flight with the barf bag clutched to his chest. It hadn't helped that he smelled like stale pizza.

Thankfully, he'd managed to keep his stomach contents inside, but I still felt the need for a good, hot shower to sanitize myself.

With a fresh towel from the linen closet that Katie's cute and somewhat cantankerous nanny had pointed out, I headed into the Jack and Jill bathroom that I'd once shared with Liam.

After a fifteen-minute shower, I felt like a whole new person. I dried off and wrapped the towel around my waist and stepped out. The mirror was fogged, so I opened both doors to air out the room.

I pushed open the door that led to Liam's room and paused.

No longer was it the carbon copy of my old room. Instead of blue paint, it was white. The bed in the middle of the room had a floral comforter haphazardly strewn across it. There were a few pieces of clothing on the floor—as if someone had gotten dressed in a hurry. Makeup was scattered across the dresser, and a curling iron was plugged into the outlet. This was definitely not something Liam would have left to gather dust.

Confused, I walked around the room, trying to figure out who lived here. Last I knew, the entire McKnight clan had moved out. Not that it would stop them from throwing a huge family party. In fact, the reason for the party might just be that the McKnights wanted their kids all under the same roof again. I was mighty glad they'd included me on the guest list and felt bad for not getting back here sooner.

But none of that explained who lived in this room.

"I'll be right back, Katie." the nanny's voice sounded from the hallway beyond the shut door. "I'm just going to get something real quick."

Panicked, I glanced around, looking for a quick escape. I was in a towel, and she was a fan. It didn't take a genius to add up the number of likes she'd get on her Insta post if she caught me. I wouldn't put it past her to have waited for this moment; especially after her comment about me making the bed and posting before and after pictures.

I was too far away from the bathroom to duck in there, and I was way too big to try to shove myself under the bed.

Standing half-naked in the bedroom of the hired help didn't look too good either.

Before I could make a decision, the latch clicked and the door swung open. Her eyes went wide, and her cheeks flushed at the sight of me bare chested and barefoot in her bedroom.

"Wh-what are you doing here?" she asked, tucking her hair behind her ear as she glanced around.

Hoping to come across as confident, and not completely mortified that I was standing in this stranger's room in only a towel, I laughed as I crossed my arms over my chest. There was a part of me that was attempting to look nonchalant…and maybe a part of me that knew folding my arms caused my chest to flex.

Sue me; she was cute.

"I think I'm a little lost," I said, taking note of the lingering gaze the nanny shot my direction. I smiled. Touchdown. I worked hard for the body I had. And I wasn't embarrassed when women appreciated it.

The nanny scoffed as she dropped her gaze and made her way over to the dresser to fiddle with the items there. "I doubt very much that you're lost," she said as she picked up a tube of what looked like lip balm and pulled the lid off.

I tried not to watch her as she ran it across her lips. Her very pink and very full lips. Instinct took over and I found myself licking his own lips. My eyes traced the gentle curve of her hips. Under that big tee shirt was a tight little bod—I'd bet my first year's salary on it.

And then, feeling like a complete idiot for staring, I stepped forward and extended my hand. "Can we start over? I didn't catch your name."

The nanny glanced down at my hand and then back up to meet my gaze. She paused and then sighed as she capped her lip balm and set it back down on the dresser.

"You are...?" I tried again, wiggling my fingers as if that was going to entice her to shake my hand. She was playing hard to get. What she didn't realize was, I always played to win.

She sighed and then gave me a smile as she met my gaze. "Not interested."

With that, she sidestepped me and made her way out to the hallway, closing the door behind her.

Now alone, I furrowed my brow as I ran my hand through my damp hair.

Well, that hadn't gone any better than before.

Somehow—and I wasn't sure how—I'd managed to tick off the nanny.

Normally, it wouldn't bother me to have caused waves. After all, I had a sea of women who would jump at any opportunity to take a photo with me. Or to shake my hand. Everywhere I went, ladies threw their phone numbers my way.

They'd thrown their actual phones and even their underwear.

Thank goodness the last one didn't happen as often as people thought it did. I'd endured week-long teasing from the defensive line because of it. Every time I walked into the locker room, underwear rained down on me. Sweaty men's underwear.

What did it matter if one girl wasn't instantly in love with me? Or that I hadn't been able to flirt my way out of this situation?

But there was something that bugged me—if she didn't like me that much, then why the Wolves shirt? Maybe she was already in love with Liam and was perturbed that I was here and Liam wasn't. Or she could have been a DuBois fan. It wasn't my fault DuBois was kicked off the team for steroid use. I just happened to be the guy lucky enough to slide into his spot.

This one girl shouldn't bother me like she did. She was the nanny, and I was here for some R & R before I returned to a life as an NFL player. That was it. There was nothing more to the situation or between us. My heart had pounded because I'd been caught in her room, not because I thought her hip would fit just right in the palm of my hand.

I scrubbed my face as I made my way back into my old room and shut the bathroom door behind me.

Desperate for a distraction, I dressed in jeans and a tee shirt and then made my way out onto the balcony, where I settled into the chair that faced the backyard.

A white tent had been set up on the grass, and people were coming in and out of it, carrying trays and speakers. The McKnights spared no expense when it came to throwing a party or building a house. Their ten-bedroom mansion sat in the middle of fifty acres. To say the McKnights were rich was an understatement. Most of the bedrooms had private balconies, en suite bathrooms, and big screen TVs. They were perks I'd definitely enjoyed in high school, but now it felt like I was staying in a high-end B&B.

Maybe in a couple days I'd settle in.

Liam's parents had hearts as big as their wallets. They took in every stray they came across, and I was no exception. I was grateful that they'd allowed me to stay with them when my parents left and never looked back.

I looked up to Joseph and Brenda McKnight as an example of the kind of parent I wanted to be one day. A day far in the future, for sure. They'd helped me realize my dream of playing in the NFL by coaching me through my college essays and applications. They'd taped my games to send to coaches and to post online for recruiters. They even bought me sheets and a new blanket, which Brenda had used to make my bed when they dropped me and Liam off at college.

All I got from my bio parents were phone calls on holidays and a Christmas card every year. Sentiment wasn't something that ran strong in the Jagger household. As much as I wanted to tell myself that I didn't care...I did.

Growling, I shifted in my seat as I pushed down my rising emotions. I hated how weak they made me feel. They reminded me of what I wanted, what I didn't have—a place to call home and a family to go with it. The McKnight mansion was as close to home as I could get, but most days, I felt as if I didn't really *belong*.

Voices echoed below my balcony, and I straightened to see Katie emerge. She ran across the brick patio toward the grass, her curly blonde hair flowing behind her. She giggled as she dipped behind a huge planter and crouched down.

"Katie!" the nanny yelled as she came into view.

I took this moment to study her. She was disheveled, no doubt from running after Katie, but she was beautiful. Her skin was pink from exertion, and the smile across her lips was wide. She looked happy, and I couldn't help but feel jealous. I wasn't sure when the last time was that I'd felt truly happy.

Exhaustion hit me like a brick wall, so I pushed up from my seat, made my way back into the room, and shut the balcony door behind me. I'd had enough of walking down memory lane. I needed a nap before the festivities later.

I also needed to get my head on straight before I came face-to-face with everyone from my past.

After all, I was Jaxson Jagger. *Sports Select* had proclaimed me sexiest football player—in both meanings of the word—of the year.

I had an image to uphold.

Getting all emotional and lonely wasn't part of that image.

Neither was obsessing over a nanny.

"I should have known I'd find you lounging around up here." Liam's voice cut through the hazy fog of sleep.

I turned toward the voice only to have something heavy and hard fall on top of me. I grunted as instinct took over and I curled up to protect my body.

"What the—"

"Wakey wakey," Liam said, flipping on the light.

I glanced up to see that Liam had thrown his suitcase right on top of me. I growled and shoved it off. It thumped to the ground. Not wanting Liam to throw anything else on me, I scrambled to get out of bed.

"Took you long enough," I said as I reached my hand out. Liam studied me for a moment before he clasped my hand and pulled me close. We pounded each other's backs.

"Oh, you know Violet. Always making a scene when I leave," Liam said. Violet was Liam's a-little-too-clingy girlfriend. She was attending a summer session at the University of Texas at Austin, so couldn't come home with him.

Which I was grateful for. To say that my personality clashed with hers was an understatement. She was high-pitched and whiny. But I cared about my best friend's happiness, so if Liam wanted her around, I was going to continue biting my tongue.

"Party's starting downstairs. Ma sent me up here to change and wake you up," Liam said as he grabbed his backpack and started toward the door.

I parted my lips to ask him why the heck the nanny was staying in his old room, but before I could get the words out, Liam was gone.

Not wanting to disrespect Brenda, I rubbed my face—forcing myself to wake up—and made my way over to the bathroom. Making sure that the nanny was nowhere around, I shut both doors, splashed some water on my face, and brushed my teeth.

After styling my hair with gel, I headed back into my room, where I pulled out a dark-blue button-up shirt and some black slacks. I slipped on my shoes, spritzed myself with cologne, and made my way out.

The feeling of dread I'd had was gone, replaced with excitement. Liam's siblings were like my own. They always made me feel welcome. And Liam's kid sister, Charlotte, well, she'd always had these goo-goo eyes for me. I needed a pick-me-up from the nanny episode earlier today. Charlotte was adorable.

I shook my head. My best friend's little sister, and the youngest of the McKnight family, was off-limits. The last time I saw her, she had freckles, braces, and frizzy blonde hair.

Realizing that I was spending a little too much time thinking about Liam's kid sister, I pulled out my phone and leaned against the wall as I texted Liam. There were so many closed doors on the second level, and I wasn't sure which one Liam was behind.

Jaxson: Ready and waiting, Cinderella.

I sent the text and then waited. A second later, the third door on the left opened, revealing Liam in a black button-down shirt and khakis.

"Cinderella? Seriously? May I remind you that you were the one that made us late to the Met Gala. Something about getting your hair just right?" Liam said as he passed by me, reaching his hand up to tousle my hair.

I anticipated it and dodged out of the way. "Hey, I've got an image to uphold," I said as I touched my hair to make sure it had stayed put.

Liam chuckled as we made our way down the stairs. "Yeah, yeah, yeah."

When we got to the bottom, I glanced around to see who had come. Most of the attendees were familiar—granted, they were older than I remembered. All of them were residents of Evergreen Hollow. No one missed an opportunity to go to a McKnight party.

It didn't take long to spot Carter, or I should say Dr. McKnight, the man of the hour. He stood by the door, greeting the partygoers as they came in.

In the background, I could hear Brenda organizing the servers in the kitchen. She was tiny but formidable.

"I heard you, I heard you," a soft and now familiar voice said from behind me.

It was annoying, but my heart picked up speed as I turned; excited that the nanny had stayed. Maybe this time, I'd actually get some information from her.

I wasn't prepared for what I saw. I almost choked on my own spit as my gaze combed over the image in front of me. The red dress hugged all the right places. Her blonde hair was down and fell in soft ringlets around her face. Her bright blue eyes widened and sparkled in the evening light.

She blinked a few times as her gaze ran over me. I may have been imagining things, but I swear she blushed.

"Lottie," Liam said, stepping into view and engulfing the nanny in a hug.

My ears rang. Confused, I glanced between Liam and the girl he'd just called his sister's nickname. Did they hire someone with the same name?

"Lottie? Like Charlotte? What are the odds?" I said, cursing the pitch of my voice. What was I, a teenage boy again?

Liam furrowed his brow. "What are you talking about?" he asked while keeping his arm wrapped around the shoulders of the nanny. She looked up at him with a heavy dose of admiration. His possessive nature confirmed my earlier thoughts that the nanny had a thing for my best friend. Well, that cleared up why she was so cold earlier. She'd wanted me to be Liam.

Now that I understood, I could extend a hand of friendship instead of flirting with her. Maybe she'd be the key to getting rid of Violet. That was a plan I could get behind.

Realizing that Liam was still staring at me with a confused expression, I said, "Your nanny has the same name as your sister? What are the odds?"

Liam held my gaze for a moment before he busted out laughing. "Man, it has been a long time. Jaxson, this is Charlotte. Lottie," Liam said as he squeezed Charlotte and then let her go.

I blinked a few times as my brain finally registered what Liam had said.

The gorgeous, way-too-sexy-for-her-own-good *woman* standing in front of me was Liam's little sister?

Well, crap.

3

LOTTIE

*T*he appreciation in Jaxson's green eyes had been worth the hour and a half of hair products, heat, makeup, and body scrubbing I'd gone through. When his gaze slid down my body in a slow, smooth way, I silently blessed the designer of the red dress for sharing their talents with the world. There was no way I could get his attention while sporting a cleaning getup and spastic hair. But now? Now, he noticed. Now, he would regret kissing me and then completely blowing me off.

It drove me a little nuts that he didn't look so bad either. The fitted, dark-blue button-up shirt made his skin look warm and touchable—and I knew how touchable his skin was. Just seeing him standing there with a stunned expression transported me back to my room when I saw him earlier with nothing on but a towel and a sexy smile.

Apparently, I have a vivid memory because just the thought made my cheeks flush and my entire body heat up. If I was hoping for the upper hand, I was rapidly giving away my advantage.

In an attempt to gain control, I shoved the image away. A woman couldn't be expected to unsee something so divine, but now wasn't the time to dwell on Jaxson's physical perfection.

"Lottie? Charlotte?" Jaxson blinked a few times as if he were still unsure of what he'd heard. "Your little sister?"

Liam glanced between the two of us as if he were trying to read the next play on the field. Thankfully, he didn't know there was a history between us. If there was one thing I knew, Liam didn't mess around when it came to his friends and me. I was off-limits. Period. Jaxson wouldn't have told him about how he stole my first kiss, and I sure as heck wasn't going to spill the beans.

"Yeah. Crazy, huh? Imagine how old this makes us look to have a little sister so grown up," Liam said as he reached out and punched Jaxson in the shoulder.

"I don't believe it." Jaxson grabbed a cup of punch off a passing tray and threw it back.

I had the urge to touch my hair and make sure it was all in place, but I forced my hand to stay casually draped at my side. Let him stress, this was my moment to be the superstar.

Liam chortled. "Believe it." His arm around my neck tightened, and I instantly flashed back to years of noogies. I hurried to shove him away before he messed up my hair that had taken hours to perfect.

"She graduated last spring," Liam continued as if I weren't standing there.

Though Liam's voice was full of pride, he was making the situation worse. Nothing said "all grown up" like moving back home after graduating college. I hurried to add, in a calm and confident voice, "I'm looking for a nutritionist job. They're not easy to come by."

"And here I thought you were just the nanny." Jaxson set his empty cup on another passing tray.

Liam laughed. "The nanny? Why would you think that?"

Jaxson shrugged as he took another glass off a nearby tray and drained it. "She answered the door earlier with Katie. What was I supposed to think?" He seemed to have collected himself and, once again, assumed the know-it-all tilt to his chin.

From what I remembered about Jaxson—well, before he kissed me —he was always in control. He must feel like he was on even ground again now that he had me locked into a place he could handle.

19

And I hated being handled. Call it a baby-of-the-family thing, but nothing grated against my skin like being *handled*. Also, *just* the nanny? What was wrong with a woman who took care of children? Had he really been so close-minded, so egotistical all this time, and I hadn't seen past his muscles to the real Jaxson underneath?

"And running head-first into another guy is somehow better?" I asked, not wanting to stoop to his level but unable to stop myself from sparring. "Watching Katie is a perk. The *best* perk," I bit out.

Now both Liam and Jaxson stared at me. I winced, realizing that I may have insulted not just Jaxson, but Liam as well. They were both NFL players. I should have known they would take offense at what I just said.

Being near Jaxson was suffocating and never in the same way. Either he was so dang hot I could barely breathe, or he acted like I was beneath him, *just* Liam's little sister, and it made me want to scream. My heart pounded against my chest.

I needed an escape. "If you two gentlemen will excuse me, I'm going to find a dance partner."

I didn't wait for them to respond. Instead, I tempered my speed as I walked away—it would do no good to look like I was running from them. That would only solidify Jaxson's impression that I was immature. I wasn't, I was in control.

Once I hit the French doors, thrown open to invite guests into the gardens and the cool evening breeze into the gathering room, I leaned against the outside wall and took a deep breath.

The white tent with a temporary wooden dance floor was half full of couples. The intimate round tables were packed. I calmed my mind as I remembered I'd promised Mom I would keep an eye on things outside.

A task seemed like the perfect distraction. I made my way to the edge of the dance floor, checking the outdoor buffet tables. They were well stocked, and I made a mental note to tell Mom the new catering staff was doing an excellent job. Next, I surveyed the faces of the guests. There were smiles, laughter, contentment, and even infatuation with large doses of flirting.

The party was a success. Mom would be thrilled.

"Charlotte!" Suzie exclaimed from behind me.

I squealed as I turned, grateful to see the pink cheeks and wild, curly hair of my best friend. She had her dark-green floor-length dress bunched up in one hand as she awkwardly picked her feet up to tromp across the grass. I could see her frustration build with every step as her heels sunk into the soft ground.

"Why does it always have to be outside?" she asked.

I rounded the table and pulled her into a hug. I needed this. I needed my friend. "I'm so happy you're here," I said as I squeezed her.

Suzie made a choking sound like I was suffocating her, so I pulled back. She wiggled her eyebrows in my direction. "Is it that bad?"

I nodded.

"Let me get some food and you can tell me all about it." Suzie upto the table, and I helped her grab a plate. Once it was stacked high with coconut shrimp and tiny quiches, we made our way over to one of the empty tables and collapsed.

Suzie started eating, so I took her silence as my opportunity to talk. I leaned back against my chair and let out a sigh, releasing about half the anger lingering in my blood. Then I recounted every detail from the moment I opened the door and saw Jaxson to his blatant dismissal of me as the younger sibling. When I was finished, I leaned forward and rested my elbows on the table.

Suzie had finished most of her food and used the small square napkin to wipe her fingers. She flagged down a waiter and grabbed a fluted glass. "Man, I wish I had been there to see Jaxson's face when he saw you for the first time." She waved her hand in my direction as she downed her drink. "Show it to me again?"

I imitated Jaxson's shocked expression and sent Suzie into a fit of giggles.

"Oh, man, that's priceless. Mr. MVP, too-sexy-for-his-own-good Jagger, stunned speechless by my girl." Suzie reached out to tap my knee.

I rolled my eyes. Suzie had never approved of my crush. She'd always told me that Jaxson would break my heart. When he did, after he kissed me, she'd been kind enough not to say she told me so. Instead, she bought me ice cream and all the Ryan Reynold chick flicks that existed.

Ready to change the subject for a minute, I asked, "Dr. Johnson let you out early?" I leaned forward to steal a shrimp from her plate. Suzie worked for Evergreen Hollow's veterinarian. He was old and cranky but had a soft spot for Suzie.

Suzie shot me a *girl, please* look. "What do you think? He wasn't too thrilled, but I've got that man wrapped around my finger." She stuck up her pinkie and wiggled it. "He's like my long-lost grandpa. I think he keeps me around 'cause I help him stay young."

I snorted as I sipped a drink that I'd snagged from a nearby tray. "What?"

Suzie had a mouthful of shrimp. "You know all the articles about how if grandparents take care of their grandkids, they live longer? I think that's what I'm doing for Bert."

I shook my head as I reached out and fiddled with the floral centerpiece in the middle of the table. "I think they're talking about little grandkids. You're an adult."

Suzie shrugged. "Eh, I don't think there's an age limit." Then she waved away my comment. "Let's talk about how you're going to get back at Mr. Forgetful?"

I stared at her. "Oh, right. Jaxson. I'm thinking…not?" I wasn't really the revenge type. Or the showy type. Or the make-a-scene type. I was already halfway resigned to life as it had always been with him.

Suzie sighed. "You're so lucky I'm your friend. What would you do without me?"

I smiled. She was right. I'd be a wallowing mess right now if not for Suzie. We were like ying and yang. I tempered her sporadic nature with some good old common sense, and she kept me from a life of drudgery.

Suzie finished her last bite and then pushed her plate away. "Okay, what's the one thing a man wants and will drive himself crazy over?"

I stared at her. If she knew the answer to that question, why wasn't she filming a course and selling it online? Seriously. "I don't know."

She sighed as she realized that she was going to have to walk me through this. "A woman he can't have. We have to make you the most irresistible person to him but show him he can't have you." Suzie straightened as she glanced around. Then she quickly glanced back at me. "Don't look now, but Jaxson is headed over here right now."

My body instantly heated as I stared at Suzie in fear. "What do I do?"

"Take a deep breath. You've got this. You need to blow him off. Whatever he has to say, you laugh, ignore, and walk away." She stared at me. "Can you do this?"

I chewed my lip as I attempted to calm my nerves. "Laugh, ignore, and walk away. I can do that."

"Yes, but that's not all."

I felt my resolve floundering. "It's not?"

Suzie shook her head. "Once you know you have his attention, once you've blown him off, then you need to find someone else to flirt with." She straightened. "He's almost here. When I say go, get up and walk away from the table. Make him chase you."

My heart pounded as I nodded along with every word Suzie said. I was pretty sure I looked like a bobblehead, so I tried to tone down my reaction. I knew she hadn't given me a ton of instructions, but Jaxson's impending arrival had my brain short-circuiting, and I couldn't remember them all. Laugh and...something.

"Go, now," Suzie whispered as she practically shoved me from my chair.

Not really sure where I was going or what I was doing, I took off toward the food table, where I nervously adjusted the napkins. I felt like an idiot as a sweet old couple had to bypass me to get to the plates.

I apologized and started to make my way back over to the table, ready to call it quits, when a warm hand on my arm startled me.

I whipped around to find myself up close and personal with Jaxson once again. The scent of his body wash, all spice and man, filled my senses as it had earlier in the bathroom we now shared. My skin tingled from his touch, and it angered and exhilarated me at the same time.

"Couldn't find a partner?" he asked, lifting one eyebrow in question.

"I haven't applied myself to the task, thank you very much." I lifted my chin, reveling in the sudden urge of confidence that shot through my veins. I don't know what Suzie had done, but I suddenly felt unstoppable. Like this was my moment to show Jaxson Jagger that you don't just kiss Charlotte McKnight and walk away.

"I can save you the trouble." His fingers slid down my arm, and he grasped my hand. My skin lit on fire and my pulse thrummed through me like the increasing tempo of a song. Realizing that I was losing my hold on the situation, I stepped back. "Trust me, finding a dancing partner isn't the problem."

His gaze dropped to me, and the intensity in his green eyes did crazy things to the butterflies in my stomach.

He stepped closer. "Why didn't you tell me who you were?" He searched my face.

For a moment, I wondered if he was looking for hints of the girl I once was or something else. I hated myself for wanting it to be more. This live wire of attraction I felt had to have another end. Could he feel it too? Did I want him to?

"Would it have made a difference?"

His eyes tightened and he dropped my hand. Without him saying a word, I knew the answer. It was the one I'd feared ever since he kissed me and walked away. I was never going to be more than Liam's little sister to him. I was forever burned into his mind as a braces-wearing annoyance that he once threw popcorn pieces at in our home theater. I was never going to be the princess in his fairytale life.

In an attempt to maintain some sort of dignity, I took a step away, straightened my shoulders, and smoothed my features into a sultry smile. "You should mingle."

"What are you going to do?" he asked with a note of panic.

"I'm going to dance." I managed to sound confident even if that was the last thing I felt. I sauntered away, hoping he was getting an eyeful of the dress and the way my legs looked in my heels.

I wasn't sure where I was going, all I could think about was what Suzie had said. A man can't stand it when he can't have a woman. I had to make myself unavailable. But how?

Thankfully, Jeff Dearden stepped right into my line of sight a moment later. I almost kissed him on the spot. We'd been good friends since middle school. Since I freed him from his locker and made up an excuse for the both of us being late for class.

I didn't fight the huge smile that emerged. Adulthood had done great things to his physique. He was the perfect person for me to make Jaxson jealous with.

Good old Jeff. He owned the sporting goods shop in town, and last I knew, he was still single. The perfect solution.

I grabbed his arm, and his face lit up in recognition. "Lottie, how are you?" He hugged me quickly.

"Great. Jeff, it's good to see you." I resisted the urge to look over my shoulder to see if Jaxson was watching. I was going to give Jeff my full attention and put that over-muscled man out of my thoughts.

He glanced quickly at the drink in his hand and set it down on a table. "Want to dance?"

"I thought you'd never ask." I hooked my arm in his, and he led me onto the dance floor just as a slow song started up. I squealed when Jeff spun me around and then wrapped his arm around my waist.

"I didn't know you could dance like this," I said, glancing up at Jeff. My emotions were so out of whack, that my pulse felt as if I were going into cardiac arrest.

Jeff glanced down and smiled at me. "A lot can change with time, Lottie. Even dorky, two-left-feet kids." He gave me a wink and spun me out again.

Even though I didn't want to, I took the opportunity to look for Jaxson, but he wasn't where I'd left him.

A stab of disappointment shot through me, but I didn't have time to dwell on it too much. After all, I was dancing with Jeff, and he seemed more than eager to give me his undivided attention. Even Suzie was shooting me a thumbs-up from her table.

I sighed, wanting desperately to push thoughts of Jaxson from my mind, but it proved more difficult than I anticipated. Which I should have known. After all, it had been years since I'd seen Jaxson, and yet, I could still remember what it felt like to feel his body against mine. To feel his lips pressed to my lips.

But it was futile, hoping that something could happen between us. He was Liam's best friend. He was forbidden. And most of all, he was never going to see me as someone other than his best friend's annoying little sister. No amount of wanting or wishing on my part was going to change that. Acceptance was my only path to healing. Once I had that, I could move on.

Hopefully.

4

JAXSON

I stood just inside the French doors, tucked to the side where Lottie wouldn't see me, watching her dance with that stupid Jeff Dearden. The man was insufferable, acting like he was king of the small town and Rico Suave because he'd put on 40 pounds of muscle and ran a business. Big deal. I could buy five businesses on Main Street if I wanted to and could lay Jeff out flat. Money didn't make the man. And muscle didn't make a mouse into a lion. Just ask my father. No amount of football success had gotten me so much as a "good job" out of the old man.

I stared down at my drink. My relationship with my father was a train of thought better left on a sidetrack. What I wanted was to spin Charlotte around the dance floor and feel her in my arms.

A memory flashed in my mind. One that was soft and sweet, innocent really. I was wrapped in a warm light, Lottie's light. I had the feeling that I'd tasted her goodness before, and it was more than I could handle.

She had certainly turned into more than I could handle. Where had her attitude and confidence come from? The Lottie I remembered was quiet and shy—cute as a button back then. Even with braces and braided hair, I'd known she'd be a looker one day. Her potential had been all over that heart-shaped, teenage face. Now look at her. The light I'd glimpsed back then had become a beacon that drew me to her. I should walk away—keep a level of distance between us.

But I couldn't leave my spot at the door. Not while she laughed all carefree and flirty with that jerk, Jeff. Jeff! What did she see in him?

I'd royally messed up with Lottie. We could have been friends. But there was this weird thing going on inside of me—a war of sorts. One side clearly remembered the reserved girl who moved like a ghost through the house, hardly saying a word. She was so innocent, so *young*. It was easy to see her as a little sister.

But that red dress…

That's what started this war. I didn't look at that dress and see anything that said little sister. No sir. That dress, and the curves inside it, had a whole other vocabulary. I didn't want to notice those things about Lottie. It wouldn't do anyone any good. But I at least needed to make nice with her. The McKnights were the closest thing to family I had, and I didn't want to screw that up.

I had trouble in my room today, reconciling who I was seven years ago and what happened with who I was now. Lottie must be mixed up in all that somehow. All these thoughts and feelings were just my brain trying to process. I needed to stop worrying so much about it.

Usually I had game. I charmed beautiful women all the time. Models, actresses, heiresses, and princesses had found me irresistible. But a hometown beauty? She brushed me off like dead leaves stuck in her cleats. Annoyed, I shifted my weight and jammed my hands into my pockets.

"Hey, Jaxson," called Mr. McKnight.

One of the few voices that could tear my eyes away from Lottie was her father's. I knew better than to mess with the head of the McKnight clan. I turned away from the couple on the dance floor and gave my host a cover-worthy smile. Hopefully, he hadn't caught me staring at his daughter. While I was pretty sure he thought of me as an adopted son, I wasn't sure he'd appreciate me paying too close atten-tion to his baby girl. He'd always been protective. "Yes?"

"I'd like to introduce you to a friend of mine, Mayor Thomas."

I nodded, ready to do my part to make the party a success. It had taken some time for me to get used to the idea that, as a celebrity, people thought they could ask for anything. Not that Joseph McKnight was like that. But the mayor probably was. It was all part of the price of being great at what I did. Sure, there were NFL players that flew under the radar, but they also didn't get playing time. General managers liked a player who was willing to put a face to the team. My agent had sold me as that kind of a player.

"Hello." I held my hand out.

"Jaxson Jagger!" Mayor Thomas was a barrel-chested man with a salt and pepper goatee. He pumped my hand and slapped my back like I was one of the good ol' boys coming home the conquering hero. I couldn't lie, it felt good. Dang good. I looked around, hoping Lottie was within earshot. She may have brushed me aside, but not everyone was annoyed I was here.

"You know, Jaxson, I've been looking for an emcee for our annual fundraiser for the children's hospital wing. You're just the guy I'm looking for."

I immediately liked the idea for several reasons. The first one, I had a soft spot for sick kids and spent my free time in Austin volunteering in children's hospitals. Children were so honest. Sure, they were starstruck when I walked into the room, but they didn't treat me any different than a regular guy, and they'd tell me if I messed up on the field. Or, if I said something dumb, they teased me about it. I always knew where I stood with kids, and it was freeing.

The second reason emceeing was a good idea was that I could use the tax write-off. My accountant would love it if I waved my normal speaking fee. And, from the way the mayor was fidgeting with his napkin, I got the feeling they didn't have the budget to get a big name.

"Absolutely." I took one of my agent's cards out of my phone case. "Give this guy a call and he'll set it up." I made a quick note in my phone to text Brent that I'd already agreed to the event. My calendar for the off-season was blessedly empty, so I wasn't worried about dates.

The mayor glowed. "Well, this has been a productive night, wouldn't you say so, Joe?"

Joseph laughed. "If I'd known you were going to ambush him, I'd have told him to run."

We all shared a laugh, and I sank a little deeper into the cushion of being with people who valued me and what I did. I asked how long the charity had been in place. Just as the mayor was about to fill me in, a cry of pain shot through the open doors. It raced through my veins like cold lightning, and I was outside before my brain caught up to my feet.

Lottie was on the floor, her shoe off to the right like it had been thrown off by an impact. My heart dropped at the sight. I'd seen shoes come off in practice, and on the field, it meant injury—sometimes game-changing injuries. I both panicked and zeroed in on the situation with the laser focus that had taken me to the top of my game.

"I'm so sorry," Dearden bent over Lottie.

Lottie glanced around at the gathering crowd of neighbors, friends, and acquaintances gawking at her on the ground. She dropped her eyes, avoiding their stares.

All I could think about was getting her out of there. She didn't like the spotlight, and she shouldn't have to endure it just because Dearden didn't know how to keep a woman safe.

She winced and gently touched her ankle. I dropped my gaze and instantly knew she wouldn't be walking on that foot anymore tonight. She might not even be up and around tomorrow. What she needed was elevation and ice, pronto.

I rammed into Dearden with my shoulder, bumping him out of the way.

See? mouse.

Without a word, I bent over, scooping Lottie into my arms and standing. She fit perfectly. Like, I could see myself carrying her across mud puddles and football fields and thresholds for the rest of my life. Was that something I wanted? I didn't know. I was running on instinct and adrenaline and a need to keep her safe and as far away from the likes of Jeff Dearden as possible.

"Put me down," she gasped, grabbing at the hem of her dress to pull it over her stunning legs. The sight of them momentarily stole my breath away. The red dress was a hot little number. But her skin? Her skin was awe inspiring.

"Hey!" Dearden straightened himself out, tugging his tie back in place and re-tucking his shirt. Seriously? I hadn't bumped him *that* hard. "I can take care of her."

"Wrong. You're the one who broke her," I answered through gritted teeth. If he knew what was good for him, he'd tuck tail and run. I wouldn't even have to put Lottie down to lay him out. With the adrenaline coursing through my veins, he'd be an idiot to push me.

"I didn't break her," he fired back.

"I slipped," Lottie said. She put her palms on my chest and pushed. Which did nothing. "Jeff, I'm so sorry."

I glared at him. There was no need for her to apologize to Dearden.

"No, I'm sorry." Dearden stepped forward. "Didn't see the edge of the dance floor. I should have been watching."

Yeah, you should have.

"It's my fault," Lottie insisted.

I almost gagged. Were these two going to apologize all day long? How could they not see they were so wrong for each other? Who wanted a lifetime of having to be tearoom polite?

"You're sorry, he's sorry. We're all sorry. There. Better now?" I resituated my hold on her and spun away from Dearden.

"Put me down," Lottie hissed while avoiding eye contact with the people around us. I couldn't see them. Didn't know or care who was watching at the moment. All I could see, all I could feel was her and the river of attraction gaining power. I shouldn't have picked her up. The war inside of me shifted in favor of the "Lottie is a woman" side.

Setting her down was impossible; her foot wouldn't be able to hold her weight. "I'm taking you to bed," I said, my voice coming out husky and intimate when I meant it to be authoritative and bossy.

The gathered circle gasped. My neck flushed as I realized what I'd said. I hadn't meant it to come out so suggestive. I must have left my brain with the mayor when I ran out. I cleared my throat and kept my eyes on the woman in my arms. The view was stunning even if she was scowling at me. That was fine. I'd take her angry beauty and use it to keep us apart. The more walls she put up, the better.

"Follow me." Suzie motioned over her shoulder as she pushed through the crowd.

Thankful someone seemed to know what to do, I followed Lottie's best friend into the house. Funny, but I didn't have any trouble seeing Suzie as all grown up.

"What happened?" asked Mr. McKnight as he met us at the doors. He glanced at me accusingly and then focused on Lottie. I felt like a bug that had crawled into the bathtub—exposed and out of place.

Resigning herself to being carried around, Lottie sighed and wrapped her arm around my neck to hold on. I tipped her body so that she was pressed against me tighter and held her close. The soft scent of her perfume filled my senses and clouded my brain. Where had she sprayed it? Her wrist? Her neck? All I could think about was burying my face between her jaw and her shoulder and breathing deeply—maybe for the first time in my life.

"I fell. It's silly. If I could just get down…" Lottie tugged at her dress again.

"Her ankle's swollen." I turned her slightly to show her feet to her dad. He tsked and motioned for Carter to come over.

I could feel Lottie tensing in my arms as people glanced our way. She'd never been into drama, and it was nice to know that hadn't changed. "Let's get her upstairs." I moved to push through the small group chatting beside us, and the crowd parted. It was like they'd all been listening with one ear and just needed a signal to get out of the way. Whispers followed us like dry leaves picked up in the wind. I curved my shoulders, trying to keep prying eyes away from Lottie. She leaned into me, and my heart leapt with triumph. Maybe I'd made amends for being a blockhead earlier.

Right on the heels of applying a Band-Aid to my wounded pride, there was a feeling that I'd done something right by this woman. It was new and powerful. Strong enough to overpower my good sense and walk right into her bedroom like I knew where I was going. It was only after her family followed us in that I realized I should have played dumb.

Her dad looked at me like I'd broken a rule.

Her mom and sister rushed in. "Goodness!" Brenda fussed as she gently probed Lottie's ankle.

Okay, maybe I had broken a rule by coming in here earlier—in just a towel. I prayed Lottie wouldn't rat me out. When I glanced down at her, her lips were pressed together in a flat line. If she was thinking about this afternoon, it wasn't a good memory.

Or maybe her foot hurt.

I waited while Penny straightened the cover and arranged the pillows with all the practice of an ER nurse, already dreading the moment I had to set Lottie down and let her go. Because that's what I'd be doing. I'd have to let go of the attraction I felt. I'd have to forget the way she felt pressed against me, so right, so perfect, so real and lasting. Like forever in a tiny little package of curves and spunk.

As I laid her down, her hand slid against my neck and ruffled the hair there, sending shivers across my skin. Her one touch was like fire and ice, branding the sensation in my memory. I had a spontaneous desire to press her into the pillows and kiss her until her hair was a mess and her cheeks flushed with passion.

"Thanks," she whispered, her beautiful lips curving into a shy smile.

Our eyes met and held. I stayed there, the war inside of me battling on.

Liam tapped my shoulder. "What's going on?" he demanded.

I straightened quickly, tearing the connection between Lottie and I. "Nothing." It took a moment for me to reapply my carefree attitude. "Lottie slipped and twisted her ankle." I stepped back from the bed.

Carter was busy working Lottie's ankle in small circles and then right and left.

Penny came back with additional pillows which she placed at the bottom of the bed to elevate the sprain. Brenda had declared that she was heading downstairs to get some ice, and Joseph said he'd join her.

Mr. McKnight was there for his kids in a financial sense. But when it came to mending scrapes or having emotional conversations, he was out. Which I was okay with at this moment. The less people saw my momentary lapse of judgement, the better.

Liam talked across the bed to Suzie, getting the play-by-play of the accident.

I ran my hand through my hair, messing up all my hard work for the party. Now that I'd backed away from Lottie, I'd lost my place in the chaos.

She looked up from the bed and mouthed the words "thank you." I nodded, wishing I could sit next to her and hold her hand but knowing that was futile. Lottie was so far away I'd have a better chance of walking on the moon than I would of getting close to her—physically or otherwise.

I couldn't spoil her with fancy dinners and flowers just because or get us tickets to a concert or take her to Europe. She was Liam's sister. A McKnight. And if I wanted to have any home to come back to—ever again—I'd make sure I didn't cross the line and kiss my best friend's little sister.

No matter how inviting I found those beautifully bowed lips.

5

LOTTIE

I woke up the next morning stiff and pretty certain that my breath would peel paint off a car. Before Carter had rejoined the party, he'd told me that I wasn't allowed to put weight on my foot for the rest of the night, and if I still hurt in the morning, I was to come straight down to the hospital and he'd x-ray it. People think having a doctor in the family is great, but there's such a thing as being too cautious. As the youngest sibling, I had a lot of *too cautious* in my life.

I'd tried to tell him that I was fine, but with Penny and her nursing degree as his sidekick, it was futile to argue. All those initials behind their names gave them clout in this area that I didn't have as a nutritionist.

On top of that, the intense look in Jaxson's eyes as he'd stared at me from across the room, made my tongue freeze and I couldn't form real words. If I'd opened my lips, I would have sounded like a puppy dog with a mouth full of peanut butter.

His brow had pinched together as he soaked in every bit of instruction Carter handed out. With his jaw set like he was going to run for the end zone, I knew his knight-in-shining-armor display from earlier was going to be in effect until my ankle healed.

Still, a little jaunt to the bathroom wasn't going to kill me. I was alone and in desperate need of some mouthwash. And I needed to pee, or my bed was going to become Lake Superior.

I leaned on every surface I could as I hobbled to the door. I winced as, a few times, I had to put pressure on my injured foot. I was pretty sure it wasn't broken, and the last thing I wanted to do was spend the day in the hospital. The more I moved around, the easier it became. I went for a normal step, and the ankle gave out, sending me stumbling into the bathroom door. Great. At this rate, I'd be jogging by Christmas.

I fumbled for the handle and finally got it to turn. Just as I flipped on the light, the door to Jaxson's room opened. My entire body lit on fire as he stood there with an annoyed look on his face.

If I didn't have a sprained ankle, I would have taken off running back to bed like a kid caught looking for her mom's secret chocolate stash. There was no way in this world I wanted Jaxson to see me in day-old makeup and a crumpled dress.

All the work I'd done yesterday to convince him that I was this sexy woman was for naught. I may not be ultra experienced when it came to men, but I was pretty sure bed head and stale breath weren't going to draw him in.

"Someone's in here," I said as I leaned forward and let my hair cover my face. I felt like the old hag in all the princess movies. Give me a cloak and a poisoned apple, and I'd fit the part perfectly.

Instead of doing the polite thing and leaving, Jaxson folded his arms and leaned against the doorframe. "Good morning to you too."

The cocky quirk to his lips ticked me off. What right did he have to look all hot in his worn jeans and tight tee shirt? I didn't need his judgement. So what if I didn't wake up looking like the women on magazine covers he dated—I had class. He could take his judgements and shut them behind the closed bathroom door.

"Seriously, I need to pee, and that's not something you want to be privy to." I held my breath, wondering if laying it out there would be all it took to make him go away.

He didn't move.

Fine. He wanted to see my sea-urchin glory, then I was going to give it to him. No holding back. I growled for good measure as I glanced up.

His eyebrows rose. Ugh! He was infuriating! I glowered at him as I hobbled into the bathroom. Though my ankle continued to loosen with movement, the blasted dress that had looked so sexy last night was now twisted and bunched all weird. I attempted to smooth it down as I limped, but that caused me to lose my balance. I fumbled to grab the counter and bit back a curse.

Suddenly, a very familiar, warm, and wonderful sensation rushed through me. Jaxson's arms enveloped my entire body. His broad chest was solid to lean against. I yelped but then realized that I was breathing my dragon breath on him, so I pinched my lips shut.

If Jaxson noticed my glare, he didn't acknowledge it. Instead, he brought me over to the toilet, where he set me gently on my feet. I shifted my weight so I was standing on my good leg.

"I could have made it over here by myself," I mumbled.

He shrugged. "I'm sure you could have. But I was here. So I helped." He shoved his hands into the front pockets of his jeans and shrugged. "It's what Carter said to do." Gone was the guy who checked his hair three times before going anywhere with a camera. In his place was the Jaxson I remembered from our kiss. The one who wasn't all wrapped up in himself.

I stared at him, wanting to hit him with a witty comeback and get rid of the nice guy, but I really needed to pee. I began to squirm. "I think I can handle this part on my own," I said, nodding to the toilet.

Jaxson furrowed his brow, and then realization dawned and his face turned red. "Right. Yes." He cleared his throat. "I'll just be out there," he said, shoving his thumb in the direction of his room.

I nodded, and he closed the bathroom door behind him. I felt like I was going to burst, but I had to see what I looked like in the mirror first so I could judge the damage. The swamp lady that looked back at me winced. My hair was matted. My makeup looked like it had been applied by a big hair band in the 80s. And my dress was wrinkled and not at all elegant.

I shook my head as I shimmied my dress up and went about my business. Once I was done, I made it to the sink and washed my hands. Just as I turned the water off, there was a knock on the door.

"Are you about done?" Jaxson asked.

For the love of Pete! I glanced behind me at the door and sent a pleading look up to heaven. I knew he was being a gentleman right now, but I needed ten minutes to become human again before he saw me. Call it pride, call it vanity, call it pathetic, but when it came to Jaxson, I wanted my best self out there.

I mean, the person staring back at me was a hot mess. If I wanted any chance at having Jaxson see me as someone other than Liam's little sister, then I needed to put on a mask of eyeshadow and concealer so I could keep my distance. It was bad enough that he had this Mr. Rogers thing going this morning.

"I'm fine. I'm just going to hop into the shower," I said as I limped over to the shower door and pulled it open. The metal clanged against the glass.

Jaxson didn't respond right away. Was it wrong that I kind of hoped it was because he was uncomfortable with imagining me in the shower —in a good way—instead of disgusted?

He cleared his throat, and I paused, waiting to hear what he had to say.

"And you're okay?" he asked. His voice was deeper than I had anticipated. And it sent shivers down my spine.

"Yeah," I mumbled as I began to grasp behind me, looking for the zipper tag of my dress. I wiggled and shimmied, but nothing I did helped. That zipper tag was out of reach. I groaned. I'd had Penny zip me up last night without a care about how I was going to get the dress off.

I turned to look at myself in the mirror and contemplate my options. Any rational person would call Jaxson into the bathroom and ask him for help.

But not me. I was seriously contemplating just getting into the shower while still dressed. In fact, if I had to, I'd wear the dress forever. There was no way I was inviting Jaxson into the bathroom to unzip my dress. That was way too...familiar. My pulse couldn't handle that.

I glared at myself. "You're crazy," I said as I grabbed my toothbrush and slathered it with toothpaste. "You cannot ask him to help you," I said as I shoved the toothbrush into my mouth.

"I'm sorry, what? Did you say something?"

Man, he was not leaving. It was like he'd decided his only mission in the entire world was to help me.

Or, maybe he was afraid I'd call Jeff over. He hadn't seemed to like my dance partner all that much. The image of Jaxson bumping Jeff out of the way made me smile. It was the one and only time a man had stood up for my honor, er, my ankle as it were. I'd immediately felt bad and apologized to Jeff, hoping he understood that I was sorry for more than just falling during our dance.

I'd caught sight of Jeff over Jaxson's shoulder as he hauled me into the house. He'd motioned for me to call him. That wasn't going to happen today. Not with Jaxson standing outside my door, waiting on me hand and foot.

Now that I thought about it, Jaxson might feel a wee bit guilty. If he hadn't forgotten our kiss, then I wouldn't have had to dance with Jeff. If I hadn't danced with Jeff, then I would have never hurt myself.

If I really thought about it, this was all Jaxson's fault.

I finished scrubbing my teeth and rinsed off the toothbrush. Then I rested my hands on the countertop as I stared at myself. No grand idea had come to mind. My family was gone for the day. I was seriously stuck with Jaxson. "You can do this," I said as I narrowed my eyes. "It's just ten seconds. It's no big deal."

I inwardly snorted. Yeah, sure. Like having a totally hot football player unzip your dress wasn't a huge deal. They could auction this moment off at a charity dinner and make a bundle. I could hear the emcee now. "Ladies, Jaxson will be happy to carry you to and from the toilet and help you undress for a shower. We'll start the bidding at ten thousand dollars."

Why was I hesitating?

Because this was *Jaxson*. The man I'd had a crush on for-ev-er.

That was it—I was spending the day in the bathroom. I'd curl up on the rug and take a nice long nap, and Jaxson could stand outside that door until my mom got home.

She'd love that one. I'd get a lecture about being stubborn and prideful, and when I blushed, she'd know exactly why I didn't want Jaxson's hands on my body.

I took in a cleansing breath and closed my eyes. "Jaxson?" I called out.

"Yeah?" he answered immediately.

I shook my head as I fought my better sense. "I need your help."

The door handle jiggled but then stopped. "Is it okay if I come in?" he asked.

I nodded and then realized that he couldn't see me. "Yes," I said.

Jaxson entered slowly and looked unsure, which was strange. He'd always been this confident guy. I wondered for a moment if I'd rattled him with the whole peeing thing.

Then I pushed that ridiculous thought from my mind.

"I can't unzip my dress," tumbled from my lips like a confession.

Jaxson's entire body tensed. "I'm sorry, what?" he asked.

I swallowed and forced my confidence to the surface. "I can't reach my zipper," I repeated as I waved toward the back of my dress. I kept my face neutral—like I asked guys to do this all the time. Ha!

His eyebrows rose, and I swear his cheeks flushed. "So you want me to help?"

I nodded. "If you wouldn't mind."

He stared at me and slowly began to shake his head. "I, um...I can help."

Not wanting to drag this out too long, I turned and pulled my hair away from my neck. Then I stood there. Waiting.

It felt like we were moving in slow motion—that's how long it took for him to approach me. When his fingers grazed my skin, every point of contact heated. He paused, holding the top of my dress, the back of his fingers pressed into the sensitive skin of my neck. My breath caught and I held it.

Slowly, the zipper slid down, and the tension of my dress around my ribs loosened. I pinched my lips together and brought my arms across my chest to keep the dress from falling to the floor. I was too afraid that I would say or do something I would regret. It was best to remain emotionally blank about this entire situation. Which meant I needed to start breathing again.

A draft brushed over my bare shoulder blades and lower back, telling me the dress was completely unzipped, Jaxson stepped back. He ran his hands through his hair as he kept his gaze focused on the floor. I held the front pressed to my body and then turned around so that he was no longer staring at the clasp of my bra or—heaven forbid!— the top of my underwear.

"Thanks," I said.

Jaxson glanced at me quickly before he dropped his gaze again and shrugged. "Of course. I'm here to help."

I smiled and then glanced around, wondering if he was just being annoying or if he really didn't realize that he was still standing in the bathroom.

"I can take it from here," I said, forcing down the emotions that had risen up in my throat. There was no need to confuse either of us with my out-of-control feelings and thoughts.

This was Jaxson Jagger I was talking about. I wasn't supposed to have deep feelings for a man who my parents lovingly referred to as their sixth child.

Entertaining those thoughts only confused me. Made me feel as if I had room to hope—which I didn't. Jaxson was a heartbreaker. I was privy to his flings. I read the gossip columns. I knew that he couldn't handle a real, long-term relationship.

He was a love 'em and leave 'em kind of guy. And I knew that. He'd kissed me, and now was standing in front of me, completely oblivious to the fact that he'd broken my heart.

And I was the fool who still crushed on him.

I hobbled over to the door and waved towards his room. "Thanks," I said flatly. I needed him to leave. I needed a hot shower and soap to wash these feelings down the drain right along with my hair products and makeup.

He needed to leave so that I could work on building up a wall that was high enough to keep me safe.

Jaxson was not someone I could have a relationship with. He wasn't even someone I could *imagine* a relationship with. He was the guy on a sports poster that hung on a wall, not a real person who would make me feel special, kiss me until I couldn't breathe, and see me as his other half.

It took Jaxson a moment to realize I was dismissing him. Poor guy, this was probably a first for him. Once he did, he swallowed, his jaw muscles twitching as he nodded. Then he made his way into his room, and I shut the door behind him.

I leaned my back against the door and tipped my face upward. The word "fool" repeated in my mind like a skipping CD. I shouldn't let him get to me. If I was going to last these next couple of weeks with Jaxson home, I needed to get a grip.

I pushed off the door, slipped out of my dress, and climbed into the shower. I reveled in the heat and the water as it washed away my aches and pains from the day before. My ankle also loosened in the heat, and I was able to put some pressure on it. Once I was clean, I turned off the water, grabbed a towel, and limped out of the shower, this time not needing to hold onto the counter or the wall for support.

I dried off, wrapped my hair up in the towel, and then threw on my robe.

It was amazing how a shower changed the way I felt about the world. It was like I could see things clearer now. There was no way my family would ever get on board with us having a relationship, and there was no way Jaxson could ever see me as anything other than his best friend's little sister. I slipped on the small ankle brace my brother had left for me. Now that the swelling was down, it fit nicely.

I dressed in a pale-yellow shirt and jeans. I walked gingerly over to my vanity and tried to make something of my face. I didn't want to look like I was trying too hard, but I also wanted to remove all the images that Jaxson had of me from this morning.

I needed to look hot, but without looking like I was trying to look hot.

Once my hair was dry and styled, I threw on my flip-flops and made my way to the stairs. I held onto the bannister, hoping I could get down in one piece, only to discover that it is really hard to go down stairs with a bum ankle.

Giving up on descending with any grace, I dropped onto my behind and began to slide. When I was halfway down, I heard Jaxson shout, "Katie!" and suddenly, my niece was in my trajectory. She stood in front of the stairs, with pink cheeks and wide eyes.

"Nantie, what are you dowing?" She glanced to the left and let out her someone's-chasing-me squeal. She giggled and monkey climbed up the stairs to hide behind me.

"What are you do—"

Jaxson appeared, and suddenly, I forgot how to speak. He'd changed into a dark-green polo shirt that matched his eyes, and his hair was swept to the side, like he wanted to look like he wasn't trying but so obviously was. A small, flirty smile emerged on his lips as he folded his arms and leaned against the bannister.

"What are you doing?" he asked.

"I'm going downstairs," I said. "Where there's food."

He nodded and then leaned to the side. "That question was for Katie. What are *you* doing?"

"Hiwding," she whispered and tucked herself further behind me.

"What are *you* doing?" I asked. Watching him play with my niece was doing strange things to my insides. Talking in order to push out my confusion seemed like the best plan for me right now.

Jaxson shrugged as he shoved his hands into the front pockets of his jeans. He watched my as I slid down each step. Katie wiggled as she followed behind me like this was her new favorite game. My cheeks felt like they were on fire. Jaxson's stare was both intense and shiver-inducing.

Maybe I could slide all the way out the front door and escape.

"I'm watching Katie," he finally said when I was a few steps from the bottom.

I paused as I stared up at him. "You're watching Katie? Where's Penny?"

Jaxson shrugged. "She got a call. Apparently a patient she has is heading home today. She wanted to go in, so I offered. Besides, it was taking you forever to get out of the shower."

I scoffed as I reached the bottom step and moved to grab the bannister. Suddenly—and before I could stop him—Jaxson reached out and grabbed my hands. Warmth rocketed through my body.

I swallowed as I stared at our joined hands. Was he feeling something too?

"Let me help," he said as he pulled me up in one swift movement. I wasn't ready and flew forward. Reaching out my free hand to keep from colliding with him, my palm was now resting against his chest.

I'd been right. This man was solid muscle.

Nervous about how I felt and the fact that we'd been in this position before—though Jaxson didn't seem to remember it—I pulled back and hobbled over to the small side table that was set up next to the wall.

Katie clung to my stable leg and stared at Jaxson. I wished for a moment that I had someone to hide behind.

Not wanting to focus on my feelings any longer, I glanced behind me at Katie. "Should we get out of here?" I asked.

Before Katie could answer, a ringtone filled the silence. From the corner of my eye, I saw Jaxson pull out his phone and furrow his brow. "I have to take this," he said. He swiped the screen and stepped to the corner so I couldn't hear who he was talking to.

Worried that my curiosity would get the better of me, I twisted around and then sunk down so I was facing Katie. She had a wide, contagious grin as she reached out and placed both her hands on my cheeks.

"I wanna go to da park," she said as she squeezed my cheeks so that my lips stuck out like a fish. I nodded, made a few funny faces and then stood.

Going to the park was a fabulous idea. It meant getting out of the house. And getting out of the house meant getting away from Jaxson.

44

Katie could run and run through the playground, and I could enjoy all the amenities of a hard park bench.

With the way my body responded to Jaxson, getting out was a smart idea.

I needed some distance between the two of us. Before I did something stupid.

6

JAXSON

I tucked my phone between my shoulder and cheek and hunched my back, hoping Lottie couldn't overhear hear my conversation. "How many articles?" I asked Brent. Apparently, Lottie and I were the hottest new couple online, with pictures and articles coming out this morning. I was pretty sure she hadn't been online yet. If she had, she would have melted me with a laser glare. And, while she'd been grumpy this morning, she hadn't been hateful.

"Two. The first one's not so bad. It's more of a 'who's this woman' kind of thing. The second one had an inside source. They're claiming a lot of crap that can't be true. Tell me you're not shacking up with her. That you were carrying her off to your bedroom?"

I lifted my eyes and stared at the vaulted ceiling. The photograph from last night. I knew my instinct was right. I shouldn't have exposed her to the media like that. "I'm staying in her parents' home and so is she. We're not…" My thoughts flashed back to an hour ago when I'd unzipped Lottie's dress. Heaven help me. I didn't want to admit it, but her body was warm and her skin like velvet. If she had any idea the attraction she'd stirred inside of me, she'd run for the hills, sprained ankle and all. "There's nothing going on behind closed doors." Nothing the rest of the world—especially my best

46

friend and her overprotective brother—needed to know about anyway.

"Perfect. You've been accepted by the family and brought into the fold."

"I did that long before I was dating Lottie."

"So you are dating her."

"No. I meant before this article came out." Couldn't he hear sarcasm? "Liam McKnight is my best friend. We played on the same high school team."

"Holy crap! It gets even better. Liam has some of the best cred in the league. You get in with his sister, and your reputation as a heartless player will disappear." Brent snorted. "Sometimes you make my job so easy."

"Since when am I a heartless player?"

Brent sighed. "For about three years. Ladies know you are a two-date max. Word gets around. I'm not saying it will affect you now, but in the future, you'll have to watch out. The league is getting picky."

I clenched my jaw, wanting to fight back, but I knew it was futile. There was no sense in arguing the point. I never took a woman out more than twice. I'd learned that lesson in college. Two dates was safe; at three they got clingy and demanding. Four? Well, I'd never gotten to four. "Explain to me why a relationship fixes things."

"Fans like to see commitment. They want to know a player can follow through for them. That he's got substance. We're upping your exposure, but it's not going to do us any good if you get bad press. Make this work."

"How?" I rubbed my eyes.

"Woo her. I don't care. Do something."

I glanced over my shoulder to where Lottie and Katie were having a thumb war on the couch. They were both giggling. Katie's tongue stuck out the side of her mouth. The image was Hallmark-card worthy, and my heart thumped extra hard, like it was telling me to take a harder look at this woman.

Trust me—I'd looked harder than I should.

Reality hit me like a 350-pound linebacker. I was standing in the

McKnight home and talking about my best friend with my agent. There would be no wooing. "Liam has a strict no-dating-my-sister policy. He's chill about almost everything in the world except his family."

"Then fake it—just for a while. We can play the broken heart card after that. The fans will eat it up and excuse all sorts of things."

"Great." I wasn't thrilled with the image of me Brent painted. I had my reasons for keeping women at arm's length. Reasons I didn't need to share with him and didn't want to look at too closely. I knew I didn't have a normal childhood and was probably messed up in some ways. But, everyone was messed up. Even Liam—who had a storybook childhood—had issues. Hence his clingy and annoying girlfriend. Still. It wasn't where you came from that mattered, it's where you were going in life, and I had places I wanted to go.

"Great." Brent took my silence as agreement, which was probably a good idea because I could stand here and argue against this all day long.

"I need pics to release to the press. Stage something and get back to me." He clicked off before I had a chance to argue. I stared at my phone for a moment longer, wondering if I'd entered an alternate reality. Maybe I could press a button and get sucked back into my old life where I could date whomever I wanted and no one cared.

Who was I kidding? That was never my life. I'd just pretended like I had that kind of freedom, like I didn't care about my reputation, because I didn't want to answer to anyone. After answering to Colonel Dad for so many years, I'd gotten good at acting like I didn't care.

And really, my dating life was only partially about my image. I mean, I liked having a good public persona. I worked at it. I took great pains to ensure I wasn't photographed unflatteringly. I'd learned that lesson too. My dating habits had more to do with who I was and what I did for a living than it did about the women I asked out.

"Jaxson?" Lottie called from the couch. "We're going to the park. We'll see you later?"

I shook my head. "Nope, I'm coming with you."

Lottie shot me an annoyed look. "It's okay. You have phone calls to make."

"Nope," I replied as I shoved my phone into my pocket. "That's over, and you shouldn't drive."

She scowled.

We were off to a good start.

"With your ankle," I added.

"I know what you meant."

"Yay!" Katie cheered as she began running circles around me.

"See, Katie's excited."

Lottie reached down and pulled Katie up and onto her hip. "Katie is always excited."

"I want Jaxwon to come," Katie said as she squeezed Lottie's cheeks —something I'd seen her do quite a few times. I couldn't help but stare at Lottie's lips as they puffed out in front of her.

I shrugged as I met Lottie's gaze. She growled and set Katie on her feet before heading toward the door. She'd loosen up. Besides, some fresh air was exactly what I needed to wrap my mind around fake-dating my best friend's little sister.

But that was the problem. She wasn't so little anymore. I was dealing with a full-blown grown-up version of Lottie. This version had so much more power in her hands. She knew how to use it too. Or, maybe she had no idea how attractive she really was. That was even more disturbing. To think she'd captured my attention without trying was…unsettling to say the least.

I dug my keys out of the bowl by the front door. Dropping them there had become a habit long ago, and I'd subconsciously done it when I got back from running errands the night before. "I'll bring my car around to the front. Do you need anything from upstairs?"

She shook her head and then brushed Katie's hair off her face. "We're ready to go."

My phone beeped. I glanced down to see a link to a third article. Swear words jumped to the tip of my tongue. I glanced at Katie's big eyes and managed to keep them from slipping out. I needed to read this before I talked to Lottie about any sort of a fake relationship.

"Let's get going." I smiled easily—hiding the growing unease inside. The park. Playtime.

Read the article.

And then I might be able to ask Lottie to be my fake girlfriend.

"What in the world?" Lottie grabbed my arm and pulled my phone to her face.

A shot of something akin to fear raced through me. "It's not what you think."

She gaped at the picture of the two of us on a popular gossip site. We were looking at one another while I carried her through the crowd of people at the party. I'd known we were being recorded, but the look on my face in the picture was confusing. I couldn't remember looking down at Lottie like she was…I don't know…precious to me.

"It looks like these people think I'm your girlfriend." She shoved my hand away from her with a grunt of disgust. "I should never listen to Suzie," she muttered under the breath.

I moved to ask her what that meant, but she spoke instead.

"Did you tell them to say that stuff?"

Crap—she read fast. I'd been stealing looks at the article at red lights on the drive to the park and while we sat on a bench. I thought I was being discreet. Apparently, I didn't hide things well. "No, are you kidding? I did not tell them you were my girlfriend or that we had been together on and off for years."

"What about the part where we *live together*?" Her voice went up several notches at the end.

What was so wrong with being my girlfriend? I couldn't help but poke the bear. "Technically, that part is true."

"Ugh!" She began slapping my arm. "Fix it. I don't want the world to think I'm bimbo number 37 on your list."

"Hey." I knocked against her with my shoulder. "That's not cool."

She stopped hitting me, folded her arms, and huffed. Her eyes stayed on Katie, who was climbing the stairs to the slide for the three hundredth time. That kid loved the banana-colored spiral slide. It was two stories tall, and she giggled all the way down. Her laughter made it easy to know where she was, which was good because Lottie was in no condition to chase down the little princess.

That's why I'd come along.

I was trying to be helpful, but all I'd done is cast a rain cloud over Lottie's day. Or, judging by the line between her eyebrows, maybe worse. And, it was only going to get darker when I told her what my agent had said. "Listen, I'm sorry about the picture. These things happen when you're in the spotlight. I can't help that I'm great at football." Maybe I was subconsciously hoping she'd agree. And, maybe, I needed a boost right now.

"Funny, because I'm not currently playing for a team." She lifted her chin and looked away from me. I hated that. Hated that she wouldn't meet my eyes.

"Lottie, I'm sorry. I really am."

"Do you have any idea what this does to me?" She pointed at my phone. I clicked the button, and the screen went black. "I'm doing my best to find a job, but employers will take one look at that article and all my credibility will fly right out the window."

That was a pessimistic point of view. "Maybe not. Maybe they'll hire you because we're in a relationship."

She clicked her tongue. "Like I want to work for someone like that."

She had a point. And I didn't have a leg to stand on. But, when the score is down, you have to make big plays happen.

"Um," I started.

She whipped her head around and pinned me with a look.

Big plays, man.

"There's something else."

She rolled her eyes. "What, am I having your love child too?"

I decided to try charming and flirty, because being apologetic wasn't working with Lottie. Granted, the woman had had a rough day already, and finding out she was the topic of a national gossip column wasn't helping make it better. "As fun as that would be, no."

She smirked.

"I talked to my agent before we left the house. He's actually jazzed about the article." She continued to stare at me without response, so I stumbled onward. "Even with the somewhat scandalous slant to the article, it does good things for my image."

She made an incredulous sound in the back of her throat.

"But only because it's you," I added quickly. "You lend me a level of credibility that I've not had from the other women I've dated."

"Well, duh." She softened slightly.

"He'd like us to keep dating."

Her chin jutted back. "Keep?"

"Start? Or, more like pretend we've been dating."

"Pretend?"

I sighed. I should have let Brent explain this. He was much better at talking people into doing things they didn't want to do. Like the time he got me to work the charity car wash with my shirt off. The internet would forever be branded with images I'd rather my future children never see.

Channeling my inner Brent, I tried again. "Brent says I have an image as a ladies' man. I don't get it. I mean there are lots of guys in the NFL who don't want to get married while they play. But somehow I'm the biggest 'player' in the league."

"Wait." her fingers touched my forearm, sending heat pulsing just under my skin. "Why don't they get married?"

"Well, uh…" I stuttered. I thought she'd go after the player remark, and I had a rebuttal all ready, so I had to switch mental gears. "We have time off-season, but during the season we basically belong to the team and we aren't around much."

"So?"

"So, that can be hard on a marriage."

"Interesting. What do you think?" Her blue eyes bore into me, demanding an answer. I didn't want to say something off the cuff. This was the first real conversation I'd had with Lottie, and it was surprisingly easy to talk to her. There wasn't an agenda hanging over her, nor was there greed in her gaze. It was just her wondering about how things work in the NFL. Like a mechanic seeing a new type of engine for the first time. Curiosity was an attractive trait. "I haven't really thought about it—about getting married that is."

She dropped her arm and slouched. "So you're pro fake relationships."

"What? No." I didn't like the condescension in her tone.

"Is that what you've been doing these last few years, dating women your agent thought would help your career?"

I wished I could tell her yes; that every airhead and social media crazy woman I'd gone out with was a stepping-stone. But they weren't. I'd just thought they were pretty. Man, I was shallow. "I wasn't dating for keeps, so I wasn't dating marriable women."

"Oh." Her back straightened. Maybe she understood that line of thinking. Maybe it wasn't just NFL players who had to consider timing when settling down. Her brother Carter was out of med school and not married. Maybe he'd put things off too.

"What about you?" I asked.

"Me?" Her eyes widened.

"Yeah—do you date for keeps?"

She blew out her lips. "I'd like to."

I suddenly hated Jeff Dearden more than spinach smoothies, burpees, and two-a-day practices in the Texas heat.

"I mean," she hurried on, "now that I'm out of school, I'd like to get my career going. But, yeah, I'd like to think that there's a great guy out there whom I could spend the rest of my life with."

I wrinkled my nose. "That's such a long time."

She elbowed me in the ribs. "I'm not that young."

"Oh, I noticed." I gave her an appreciative once over. To the great joy of my manly pride, she blushed.

An idea suddenly struck. "You know, we have nutritionists in the NFL."

"Yeah? Is this your way of making me feel better? Telling me of all the people who currently have a job that I don't?" She watched Katie as she talked. "Cause it's not working."

I turned in time to see Katie wrap her legs around a fire pole. My heart lurched, and I lifted off the bench. The little squirt made it safely to the ground and took off at a sprint to the monkey bars. Sinking back down, I heaved a sigh. "Does she do that all the time?"

Lottie giggled. "Yep." She patted my knee. "The first time I watched her, I about had a heart attack."

I pressed my hand over my heart. "I can only imagine what Liam would do to me if his favorite niece was injured on my watch."

"Right?" Lottie laughed. "Liam can be overly protective sometimes."

I shook my head. "This is never going to work."

"What?"

"A fake relationship between the two of us. Your family would hang me out to dry."

She nodded. "You're probably right. But you forgot one thing."

"I did?"

"Yeah. I didn't agree to do it." She said the words so flippantly. Like there was no way on this green earth that she'd agree to fake-date me. I wasn't that bad, was I?

"Oh." I rubbed my palms together, warming up to the challenge. "What if I sweetened the deal?"

"Please don't offer to pay me."

"I wouldn't dream of it." I swallowed my first idea faster than that nasty grape-flavored cold medicine Mom used to shove down my throat before putting me on the bus, sniffles and all.

"Good."

"But I would offer to put in a good word for you with the team. A job with the Wolves would be the start for a pretty awesome career as a nutritionist."

She pressed her lips together, and I could see the wheels turning as she debated the pros and cons. I prayed the pros were much stronger than the cons, but with the length of time it took her to make a decision, I concluded that the two were neck and neck. That wasn't cool.

"Okay, so if I do this, you'll guarantee me a job with the team—as a nutritionist. Not as some intern to the GM, doing coffee runs and dusting his office?"

Man, I suddenly wanted to give her the world. "I can only promise you the interview. I don't have that much sway over the front office. There are favors I can call in to make the interview a sure thing though."

"Favors?"

"Yeah, people ask for autographs and signed memorabilia to give their family for birthdays and Christmas—stuff like that. I went to a kid's birthday party once. He was autistic and totally awesome."

She smiled. After a few visible back-and-forths in her mind, she nodded. "All right, Jaxson Jagger, I'll be your fake girlfriend, and you will get me a job interview." She stuck out her hand.

"Shouldn't we seal it with a kiss?" I teased as I puckered up and leaned forward.

Her cheeks flushed such a pretty shade of pink that it made me want to run my fingers over her skin. The thought of kissing her suddenly didn't seem so flirty. It became richer, more full of intent. "I'm kidding." I pulled back as I reached out my hand and shook hers. My palm tingled.

Katie threw herself onto Lottie's lap. "I'm hungee."

"You and me both," Lottie murmured. If I didn't know better, I would have thought she was implying something else. But I did know better. Lottie wasn't interested in guys like me. She wanted a Dearden type who stayed in town and ran a local business. Someone who would be home in the evenings 365 days a year.

I reached for Katie and pulled her onto the seat between us, draping my arm across the back of the bench. "What do you want for lunch?" I now knew why the family doted on her so much. She was so cute—I'd buy her prime rib if she asked for it.

"Pea-ut budder."

I shared a look with Lottie that said, *Isn't she adorable?* "I think I can manage a sandwich. Let's head home. I bet Nantie needs a nap."

Lottie's eyes were heavy. She nodded. "I can't believe how tired I am."

"Healing is hard work." I stood, taking Katie in my arms as I did so. I then offered a hand to Lottie.

She stood, gingerly testing her ankle while holding onto me for balance. "I can already tell a difference." She walked easier as we headed to the parking lot. "The brace helps."

Several women passed by pushing strollers. They had their cameras out and whispered just loud enough that I heard both our names. Word spread fast. Lottie stiffened.

"They probably won't approach us." I spoke low so as not to draw attention to the fact that I'd noticed the group. Once you acknowledged them, they'd think they had the green light to do and say whatever they wanted.

"How do you know?" We made it to the car, and I opened her door for her.

"Because you're here. Women usually give other women a wide berth."

She nodded. "For the most part, we respect a girl's claim to a guy. That's not to say there aren't women out there who don't care, but for the most part, we behave ourselves."

"So, it's like a girl code?"

"Total girl code."

I grinned as I opened the back door and set Katie in her car seat. Lottie was full of all sorts of information. And she was fun to talk to. I didn't remember her being this open in high school. Maybe she'd taken some time to grow into herself. She'd done a great job.

"So, I just have one question," I said as I situated myself behind the wheel. "How are we going to tell your family without getting me killed?"

She tipped her head back and laughed. "I can't make any promises."

"Great. Thanks."

7

JAXSON

"Are you counting?" grunted Liam as he pushed his arms up to complete another bench press.

Shoot. I'd lost count three minutes ago. Leading scientists say that working out is supposed to clear your mind, but mine was as cluttered as ever. Lottie. Our situation. My proposal. All of it felt suffocating.

Add in the fact that I was supposed to talk to Liam about all of this, and I was a mess. So much so that I couldn't keep track of something as simple as counting Liam's reps. And it showed. The veins popped out on his neck and forehead quite clearly.

Not wanting to admit I'd lost count, I cleared my throat and said, "Two more."

If I could wear him out before I brought up fake-dating his little sister, then I might stand a chance of getting out of here alive. And I valued my life.

I hovered my hands near the bar for safety. I was trying to make him exhausted, not break him. Coach would kill me if anything happened to one of his starters, and he was my friend. He might not think so in a few minutes, but I was sticking to our friendship until he told me otherwise.

I'd brought Lottie back to the house to take a nap and hung out with Katie for another hour before her mom got home. We'd watched cartoons, and she'd fallen asleep on the couch, holding a stuffed hippo. I'd snapped a pic. I'd never had little kids around when I was growing up, and it was kind of fun. I could see myself having a couple munchkins one day in the far, distant, way-off future.

Liam finished strong, and I had to give him props for making it through the extra reps. "Great job." I made sure the bar was on the supports before tossing a towel in his sweaty face.

He grunted his thanks and wiped down. "You're up."

I eyed the bench. The thought of pushing my muscles to the brink sounded amazing. Exercise always had a way of grounding me, and right now, I needed it. I lay down, resolving to tell Liam about Lottie as soon as we were done lifting.

"I heard you spent the day babysitting," he said as he nodded along with my reps. That was his way of keeping count. It always worked. If he stopped nodding, I would stop lifting.

"Katie's awesome." I managed to get out. Sweat pooled at my temple. Any minute now, I'd be dripping. We'd warmed up with twenty minutes on the treadmill at the super-exclusive club his dad was a part of in town. Membership fees were a bear, but the McKnights owned the building, so we'd cruised in without having to sign a six-month membership contract. Without Liam, I would have had to agree to let them post my workout on social media for advertising. Considering the storm that brewed in that area, I wanted to stay as far off the grid as possible.

"I meant Lottie." He grinned. "She can be a handful."

"Yeah…" I finished my set and dropped the bar on the supports. "About that." I sat up quickly, looking around to see if there was anything Liam could throw at me.

"Oh no, what did she do? Make you wait on her hand and foot?" He headed for the free weights.

I reluctantly followed. "Nothing like that."

"Light weight and lots of reps, or heavy weight and low reps?" he asked, already having moved on from the topic of his sister.

I needed to get him back on track and fast. "Heavy weights." He handed me a set, and I did a few half-hearted curls. Maybe I was going about this all wrong. If I built up to it—made a case for Lottie and me to run the scam—then he wouldn't see it as threatening. And if I found a way to make him feel as if he'd come up with the idea? Then it wouldn't be me asking to fake-date his sister. It would be him solving a problem.

And I liked that idea more.

"Brent called this morning. There was a new article out about me."

"Oh yeah? Anything good?" He snickered. I'm sure he was hoping for another fan throwing underwear at me article that he could give me a hard time about.

"You're not going to believe what they think." I pasted a grin on my face. "They think Lottie and I are dating."

Liam's weights hit the floor. The sound of them clanking rang through the gym like a gunshot. A guy on a treadmill nearby tripped and almost went down. One woman gasped and clutched her chest.

"What?" He glared at me, completely oblivious to the dozen sets of eyes trained on us. Great. What I should have done was wait until we weren't in public. I'd believed that having witnesses would temper his reaction. I'd been wrong.

Liam face had gone three shades of angry and his hands were in fists. I was still holding my barbells. Without taking my eyes off him, I set them on the ground. "Listen—this could be a good thing."

"In what universe?" He took a step forward. "I told you the day you moved into my house—I'll share my room, I'll share my parents, I'll even share my toothbrush if you ask. But the one thing you were supposed to keep your hands off of was Lottie."

I put my hands up. "I haven't touched her." *You know, except for unzipping her dress.* Even though that had been an act of mercy, Liam wouldn't ever see it that way. And neither would I if I were in his shoes. Which was why I banished the thought from my head—I didn't want it to show up on my face, where he'd read it like a billboard.

"Then what the—."

"It was a misunderstanding."

ANNE-MARIE MEYER & LUCY MCCONNELL

"That you're working furiously to correct." He stepped closer again. If he came into my space any more, then we'd come to blows. Yet I couldn't back down. Lottie was…well, she was the key to my new image. If I was going to fake-date anyone, she'd be a great choice. She was fun to talk to and real. I liked real. Too late, I realized I should have been saying some of this out loud.

"Actually, Brent thinks it would be a better idea to run with it—in a totally platonic way."

Liam turned his head like a cog that had gotten stuck—he couldn't quite process what I was talking about.

"We're going to fake having a relationship for a while."

He inched forward and narrowed his eyes. "Not cool. My sister isn't a pawn you can use for a publicity stunt. She's got a life of her own." He shoved my shoulder. "Are you paying her?"

"No." In that moment, I was so happy she'd refused money. I could only imagine the things Liam would call me for paying his little sister to date me, and none of them were flattering. With the hard look in his eyes, I felt bad about the barter Lottie and I had set up. I should never have asked her to do this for me. But I didn't know how to get out of it. Brent expected pics of us—and soon.

"And she agreed to this crap?"

"Yeah." My voice gave out, and I had to clear my throat to restart it. "She's on board. Happy to do a friend a solid."

"I don't believe you." He flipped around and headed for the door. I couldn't blame him. Being the girlfriend of an NFL player meant time in the spotlight, and if there was one thing Lottie avoided, it was attention.

I realized he didn't just need space, he was leaving the gym. "Where are you going?"

"To talk my sister out of the biggest mistake of her life."

Curse words shot through my mind, but I kept them to myself and prayed that Lottie wouldn't mention our deal. If Liam was going to chill, he'd have to believe that she was in this because she was helping out a friend and not because I'd bribed her into it.

We got into the car, a storm of hot anger brewing thick enough it pressed on me from every direction. "Liam, I should have talked to you first. Everything happened so fast…I didn't think—."

He slammed the car in gear and lurched out of the parking spot. "That's exactly right. You weren't thinking. This is my baby sister."

"She's not a baby anymore."

He slammed on the breaks and threw us both forward. I braced myself against the dashboard. "Dude!"

He glared at me. Without saying a word. He turned back to the road and ignored me.

I closed my eyes. It wasn't my place to make Liam see that Lottie was a beautiful, capable woman. She was so much more than just his little sister.

But I doubted that he would appreciate my interpretation of Lottie. He would only see me as a man leering at his sister. Anything I said would solidify in Liam's mind that I was doing the one thing he asked me never to do. And really, growing up, it hadn't been hard.

I glanced out the window to see the buildings rush by too fast. I needed to stop thinking about Lottie like that anyway. We'd already had enough heated interaction between the two of us to last me a lifetime.

Liam was angry with me, and I could only imagine what he would think if he could hear my thoughts. I had a feeling his reaction would involve death and a shovel. And Liam wouldn't think twice about that. There were benefits that Liam had by having a sheriff for an older brother. He could give him advice on how to take me out.

That and how to hide my body.

8

LOTTIE

The sound of my phone alarm pulled me from a much needed and appreciated afternoon nap. I rolled over in bed and stretched, wincing as my ankle shot a bolt of lightning up my leg. Apparently, a nap with no brace was not a great idea.

I guess I wasn't the naturally quick healer I'd thought I was.

I spent a few minutes lifting and lowering my foot. The pain began to subside as I stretched out the ache.

I was okay with taking my time getting out of bed and heading downstairs, where I could smell my mom's marinara sauce cooking. If she was busting out her Italian roots, that meant only one thing: my family was getting together.

Which meant every single McKnight that was currently in South Carolina was going to be here. It was the perfect time to break it to my family, gently of course, that I was going to fake-date Jaxson. Who, apparently, was the all-time greatest player of the NFL. I'd like to see the magazine cover for that award.

I sort of knew that about him. I'd read the gossip columns when I needed a break from studying. I'd seen the car wash photos—holy heck, that's an image I'll never get out of my mind. So when he told me that he wanted to date a good ole American girl, I could see it working in his favor. I just never thought I'd actually agree to go along with it.

Because for him it would be fake, but for me? Time hadn't made me forget my feelings for him, and I wasn't sure parading around on his arm, smiling for the camera would do my heart any favors. I wasn't a strong enough actress to hide my feelings. They would show up like spaghetti stains on a white tablecloth.

Three solid knocks on my door had me jolting up in bed. I glanced toward the door, wondering if it was Jaxson. After we got home from the park, he told me that he would feed Katie and put her down for a nap and that I should get some shut-eye before the big reveal.

I had to admit, I didn't fight him nearly hard enough. I was sawing some logs before my head hit the pillow.

I ran my hands through my hair, wiped quickly at my mouth, and adjusted myself on the pillows so I at least looked presentable just in case it was him. Nothing could come close to how bad I'd looked that morning, but I didn't want him to think that's how I looked every time I woke up.

"Come in," I said in what I'd wanted to be a sexy voice—but it came out choked and ridiculous.

See? Faking things is not my forte.

The door opened, and I let out a sigh. Penny stood there with her phone in hand. Her brow was furrowed as she stared down at the screen. She read out loud as she crossed the floor.

"Jaxson Jagger, no longer the mystery man? The NFL's favorite playboy has settled down with this all-American girl. Source confirms that she indeed fathered his love child." Penny looked up at me and pinched her lips as her eyebrows nearly disappeared into her hairline.

I coughed and scrambled to get out of bed. What the crap was happening right now? "Let me see that," I said as I dove for the phone and pulled it from Penny's hands.

After a quick scroll through the article, my heart sank through the floor then down through the foundation and buried itself six feet underground. "Oh my gosh. They are relentless." I could only imagine how much those nosy moms at the park got for the photo they took of us. There we were, walking along like a sweet little family, with Katie on Jaxson's hip and me holding his arm— for balance. I was holding onto him so I didn't fall over, but do you think that was in the caption? No sir.

And we looked good.

I wasn't going to brag or anything, but my yellow shirt matched the little flowers on Katie's tank, and Jaxson's polo coordinated with her dark-green shorts. I mean, if I was going to hire someone to photograph us, I couldn't have done things better.

Penny cleared her throat, and I winced as I offered her a weak smile.

"Do you mind telling me why the entire world thinks that Katie is your and Jaxson's *love child?*"

I swallowed, my throat going dry. I handed her phone back and did my best to appear unaffected. "The words 'fake news' come to mind." I turned and made my way over to my vanity and sat. I grabbed a brush to try and smooth out the sleep knots. Before I could pull it through my hair, Penny snatched it away.

"Uh-uh, there's no way you are getting off this easy. What is going on here?" She narrowed her eyes. "Are you and Jaxson secretly dating?"

I sputtered and my blasted cheeks felt as if they would burn off my face. "No," I said in the most unconvincing way possible. Seriously, I had way too much fake shock and too little disgust. So not an actress.

Penny folded her arms across her chest, causing the brush to stick straight up. "I made it very clear to Liam that I didn't want Katie in the news—I didn't think I had to spell it out for you, though. There's a reason why I won't let Dad take her places." She narrowed her eyes. "I should have realized that Jaxson would draw attention too."

Now that I thought about it, she had told me not to post any pictures of Katie on my social media accounts—in the hospital on the day she was born. It was weird, but since she'd been so tight-lipped about who Katie's father was, I didn't ask too many questions.

Then there was the time, about a year ago, when Penny was in the newspaper for coming up with a new patient-care routine at the hospital. She'd flat-out refused to have Katie in any of the pictures and insisted the article not mention her. She said it was to protect Katie from identity theft, but I wondered if there was something more to her paranoia.

"Well, I didn't want him to come to the park. He's really pushy." I started to sweat under Penny's gaze.

She suddenly let up and sighed, handing me back the brush. "I get it. You made a mistake." She walked out of my room but then paused at the door and turned around. "Just fix this. I don't need Katie to start asking me if Jaxson is her daddy."

I doubted Katie would be reading anything from *Star's Caught Red-Handed* but I wasn't going to argue with Penny if she was forgiving me.

"I promise." I made an *X* over my chest and then winced as I realized that would be a problem.

Penny must have picked up on my hesitancy, because she took a step back into the room. "What's going on with you?" she asked. "Last night you were flinging yourself at Jeff Dearden, and now these articles about you and Jaxson?" She narrowed her eyes as she walked over to me and pressed her hand to my forehead. "Are you having a mental breakdown?"

I knew she was playing with me, but I swatted her hand away. "I'm fine," I mumbled as I threw my hair up into a ponytail, and I stood before she could check my pupils or something much worse.

"There's another article you should read." She scrolled through her phone, and I braced myself for the worst.

Instead of Jaxson and I, the picture was of a charred, burned-out car. I leaned closer and read, "Sheriff Mason McKnight risks his life to save a child from a burning car." My eyes bugged out. "What in the world?"

Penny nodded. "It came out two hours ago. Mason had barely finished filing the report when the news broke. He's hiding in the kitchen, trying to pretend the world isn't calling him a hero."

"He is a hero." I scanned the rest of the article. "It sounds like he's lucky he made it out alive."

She took her phone back, her face full of love and gratitude. "He is. Mom's making pasta from scratch—she's so thankful he's okay."

I tried not to think about how dangerous Mason's job could be and chose to focus on how proud I was that he wanted to protect people and catch the bad guys. But things like this, they made me realize that he wasn't playing cops and robbers in the backyard—he was a real-life police officer who stepped in front of danger. I swallowed the lump in my throat, suddenly anxious to hug my bro and verify that he was still alive with my own eyes.

"Come on." I made my way down the stairs on my backside again, Penny walking behind me.

I marched into the kitchen and headed straight for Mason, who was busy stringing fresh pasta on dowels that Mom had placed on the counter. I ignored everyone else along the way.

He glanced up and said, "How's your—"

I threw myself into his arms and held on tight, cutting off his question. "Don't you dare ask how I'm doing. Are you okay?" I squeezed his arms and poked his chest. He'd come straight from work and was still in his uniform with his badge all shiny and bright.

He laughed. "I'm fine. Really."

"How's the boy?" I asked glancing around for Katie. Just the thought of a child in a car fire made me want to hold her close.

"He's going to be alright. They're keeping him in the hospital overnight. He took in a lot of smoke."

"But he'll be okay?" I pressed.

"Riding his bike by the end of the week." Mason's big grin filled me with comfort and eased my stress.

"Lottie's got news," Penny tossed out. Mom and Mason looked at me expectantly.

I glared at Penny. "I don't think I'm awake enough to announce anything," I mumbled. I was alert enough to talk about anything but my failing love life. The only way I seemed to be able to get a guy was if he came with a bad reputation and the relationship had an expiration date.

Which reminded me, I needed to talk to Jaxson about an end date. If I knew how long I needed to play pretend, then it might be easier to swallow.

Mom stood in front of a huge pot of sauce on the stove. She gently stirred what I'd rightly diagnosed with one sniff as marinara sauce.

"Hey, sweetie, did you sleep good, then?" Mom asked. She dropped some freshly chopped oregano into the pan and leaned over to smell the sauce. Her nose could tell when dinner was perfectly seasoned, when cakes were done baking, and when a certain daughter spilled Sprite on the carpet and scrubbed it out.

I nodded as I collapsed on the nearby barstool and rested my elbow on the countertop, setting my chin inside my palm. "Yeah, it was good."

"That was nice of Jaxson to look after Katie so you could sleep." Mom tapped the wooden spoon on the pot and then set it in the porcelain rooster holder that sat between the burners.

"Yeah, great," Penny added with a heavy dose of you're-up-to-something-and-I'm-going-to-find-out-what.

Mom turned to study me and then glanced over at Penny. "Everything okay?" she asked.

Penny sighed as she turned her phone on and then walked across the kitchen with it raised. I folded my arms and buried my face in them. It was bad enough to have the whole world think badly of me—but leave my mom out of it. After a few seconds, Mom let out an "Oh, my."

"What?" Mason asked, and before I could protest, he was across the kitchen staring at Penny's phone over Mom's shoulder.

"Love child?" Mason asked as he visibly shuddered. "Don't they realize that it would be like...incest?"

I sputtered and straightened. It was one thing to say I'd practically grown up with Jaxson and it would be weird. It was a whole other thing to insinuate that we were actually related.

Because we were very much *not* related. I had a late-night, ill-begotten kiss to prove it.

I sighed as I buried my face deeper into my elbow. If only this whole thing would disappear.

And where was Jaxson, anyway? He was supposed to help me explain all this to the family. As far as fake boyfriends went, he was unimpressive and doing a horrible job.

Mom tsked. "Mason, don't be ridiculous." I felt a hand on my shoulder. "It's not that bad. One phone call to the tabloids and it will all be over." Mom rubbed my back like that was going to solve my problems. "I'm sure Jaxson will have no problem fixing this."

"Yeah, and Liam will back him up," added Mason.

I straightened. Liam? Shoot, had he seen the article? That could explain Jaxson's absence—he'd been tossed in the ocean and left to drown. I should check the garage for the boat. I glanced at Mason, Mom, and Penny; they were now staring at me with raised eyebrows. Forget saving Jaxson, I was about to drown, myself.

"It not just that," I said.

"What is it?" Mom probed.

I took a deep breath. If I was going to tell them, now was the time. Waiting would only prolong the agony. "I agreed to fake-date Jaxson." The words tumbled out of my mouth. I hesitated as I glanced between my family members.

"So this was intentional?" Penny asked as she wiggled her phone.

I shook my head. "No. The love child thing wasn't. But the dating thing…that is. He wants to soften his image, and when the tabloids got it wrong earlier, I agreed to play along." I paused, holding my breath and anticipating their response.

Mason set his jaw—which meant he had a lot to say but was holding it back. I think that's a trait that served him well as a sheriff. He could bide his time, stew, and think things through before he spoke. I think the whole *love child* thing was more than a guy wanted to handle when it came to his baby sister. While he managed his feelings about all this, he moved back to the pasta machine to roll more dough

Mom stared at me and tucked my hair behind my ear like she'd done when I was little and crying because Tommy Middleton had pulled my pigtails. I smiled and grabbed her hand and set it on the counter. If my mom couldn't see me as an adult, I doubted the rest of my family members could either.

Penny stared at me like I had two heads. Then she shrugged and tucked her phone back into her pants pocket. "As long as Katie stays out of the limelight, I don't have an objection." Then she raised her finger. "As long as it's fake. I've read some of the articles about Jaxson. I know some things are blown out of proportion, but there's always truth behind the exaggeration." Her expression dropped, and I wondered for a moment if she was speaking about someone else. Like she knew from personal experience or something.

Her understanding wasn't as weird as her admitting that she read the gossip magazines. That didn't seem like her. Trying to keep up with what celebrities and athletes were doing wasn't her scene. She was all medical textbooks and magazines. Ever since Katie was born, I'd never seen her take a day off.

Mom was the only one who hadn't said anything, so when Penny moved to stir the sauce, I glanced over at her. Her eyebrows knit together as she stared at me.

"What?" I asked as I offered her a smile.

She shook her head. "I'm just worried you'll get hurt. I know you've always had a little crush on Jaxson. Are you sure this is just pretend?"

I groaned as I slipped off the stool and made my way over to the fridge, where I grabbed a bottle of water. "Mom, that was years ago. This is just one friend helping out another friend."

Thankfully Mom didn't follow me. Instead she stood there with her arms folded and a look on her face that told me she didn't believe a word I'd said. But after a few seconds, she raised her hands. "Well, I'm not going to stop you, but I want you to be careful. It's hard to move on from a broken heart."

"Mom, I'm not going to get a broken heart," I stammered. I'd questioned my own ability to act this out, but the fact that my family thought I couldn't handle it spurred my determination to make it work.

The garage door opened, and Jaxson and Liam's voices could be heard from the mudroom. My entire body heated. Mom reacted like a bloodhound on the scent. She raised her eyebrows as her gaze locked with mine.

I shook my head and turned, deciding to focus on dinner rather than try to sort out my feelings for Jaxson and the fact that in a few short seconds, he was coming into the kitchen with the most overprotective McKnight sibling. So far, I'd gotten off easy. But easy street had a dead end named Liam.

Had they been out together? Did Jaxson talk to him? I prayed for his sake that Mom would keep it quiet until Jaxson could break the news. I could only imagine the bloodbath if Liam was taken by surprise.

But when the two of them barreled into the house, my questions were answered. Liam knew, and he was pissed.

"Oh, good, we're all here," he said as he dropped his duffel bag on the floor.

My eyes widened as Liam stomped into the kitchen. I mean, I knew my brother had always been overprotective, but this was blowing a fake relationship way out of proportion.

My gaze fell on Jaxson, who stood near the exit. His hair was damp, and his hands were shoved into the pockets of his sweatpants. He looked stressed as he studied Liam. Then, as if he felt me studying him, he glanced over and met my gaze.

I offered him a supportive smile, but he didn't respond. Instead, he moved his gaze to Liam and leaned one shoulder against the doorframe.

Sighing, I folded my arms and turned to focus on Liam. Mom was handing him a water bottle. I could tell Liam was fuming, and it just made me angry.

"What the heck, Liam?" I asked as I marched over to him and punched his shoulder.

Liam was mid-drink and ended up spilling water down his front. He lowered the bottle and glared at me.

I wasn't going to back down. Not now. "I'm not a child, and you don't get to decide what I do or don't do and who I date or don't date."

Liam's glower deepened. "He's my best friend," he said. His voice was low.

I sighed as I stared at Liam. "I know. That's why I want to help. He's like a brother to all of us." Bleh, that word tasted gross on my tongue. But Liam needed to stop seeing Jaxson as a threat.

And it seemed to be working. He narrowed his eyes as he studied me. Then he twisted the lid on the top of the water bottle.

"What do you think, Mason?" he asked, glancing over at Mason, who was now separating freshly cut spaghetti noodles.

Mason paused and glanced over at Jaxson. I almost sighed when I saw Jaxson straighten. It was crazy, how much hold my brothers had over him. He wanted so badly to belong to our family, to be seen as an equal, to be loved. If they asked him to shave his head, Jaxson would do it.

It wasn't fair, what my brothers were doing to him. My hackles rose protectively.

Thankfully, Mason wasn't as much of a spaz as Liam. It took a him a few seconds to speak.

"Eh, Jaxson is good. He knows what we expect. I think the fear is that we'll destroy him if he hurts Lottie."

Jaxson parted his lips as his gaze swept from Liam to Mason. He looked as if he wanted to say something but then stopped himself.

"Enough," I shouted as I raised my hands. "I'm an adult and I can make my own decisions. This is happening, so you might as well all get on board." I marched over to the fridge and grabbed out a block of cheese to shred. I needed something to take my frustrations out on.

"All right, you three. Let's focus on dinner. Your father will be home soon, and I want all of this talk of fake relationships and a love child put to bed."

There was a low murmur of apology that spread through the room. Liam declared that he was taking a shower, and a few moments later, Jaxson said the same. Mom and Penny finished the sauce while Mason boiled the noodles.

I took this moment of peace to stare out the window as I shredded a mound of mozzarella. My lips tipped up into a smile as I realized I had won. I was going to fake-date Jaxson, and I was…excited.

9

LOTTIE

I stood in my bedroom, staring into my closet. A whole three days had passed since Jaxson and I declared that we were going to fake-date, and to my surprise, Liam hadn't killed Jaxson.

If anything, he seemed to grow to like the idea. Well, maybe not like it. Tolerate was more the word. It helped that Violet had shown up yesterday and put him in a good mood. She was loud and annoying, but she seemed to help Liam forget what Jaxson and I were about to do. So I endured her.

But now, standing in front of my mirror and staring at the ridiculously plain yellow dress I had on, I wished Liam had pushed a little harder for this fake-dating thing to go away. I had no idea what the girlfriend of an NFL player looked like, but I was pretty sure it wasn't a banana.

"Ugh," I said as I flung myself down on the bed and buried my face in a pillow.

"Uh-oh. What's wrong?" Jaxson's sexy and flirty voice sounded from across the room.

I gasped as I scrambled to look more ladylike. I pushed my hair from my face and glanced over to see him leaning on the doorframe that led into the bathroom. He was wearing a shirt that looked as if it were about to give up the fight; the strain from his muscles was too great. And that was all tucked into his football pants.

My entire body heated as I forced my gaze upwards. I was pretty sure my cheeks looked as if they were about to start on fire. I hated that he looked so good in whatever he wore.

I was the exact opposite.

Jaxson lifted his eyebrows as if he were expecting an answer, so I stood and brushed my dress down.

"I look like a banana," tumbled from my lips. Leave it to me to say the least sexy thing a person could say.

Jaxson chuckled as his gaze roamed over me. For a moment, I allowed myself to see appreciation in his eyes. As if looking like a banana made me tasty. And, maybe, he wanted to be the monkey who—

And my face was on fire.

"Well, it does seem a little dressy for what we're doing," he said as he stepped into my room.

I swallowed as I nodded. I was pretty sure if I tried to speak, no words would come out.

There was something different between us. Something that had changed since the moment he had walked into the house. It was as if he were finally seeing me. Like I meant something more to him than just his best friend's little sister.

And that thought excited and scared me at the same time. It left me feeling confused and jumbled. And when I felt like that, putting words into sentences became hard.

He picked up on my total lack of confidence and took charge. He wandered over to my dresser and began to pull open the drawers. I moved to stop him when he got to my underwear drawer, but he must have realized what might be inside and instantly slammed the drawer shut.

I took some satisfaction in the fact that his cheeks flushed as he swallowed. His jaw muscles clenched, and he cleared his throat.

"Maybe if you tell me what you're looking for, I can help you," I said, stepping forward.

Jaxson nodded as he stepped back. "I was thinking a pair of shorts would work."

I smiled as I pushed past him. The feeling of his body next to mine sent shivers down my back. I enjoyed it and feared it at the same time.

You would have thought I'd burned him. He jumped back and ran his hand through his hair. His Adam's apple bobbed as he squinted.

Not wanting to take offense at his reaction, I busied myself with finding a pair of cut-off shorts. I pulled out a pair that were short and cute.

I didn't want to brag, but my legs were my best feature. And I wanted to show them off. Especially since this was our first outing as a couple. Jaxson's publicist had arranged for us to go to the local high school and throw the ball around with the high school team. Reporters and bloggers would be there to document everything.

Apparently, the entire world wanted to know what girl had finally saddled America's beloved football bachelor.

Nothing like putting pressure on every part of me. They were going to judge how I looked, talked, and presented myself.

I'd already had numerous memes made out of the photos taken of us at the party. And some of them were not nice.

This was my chance to prove that I deserved to be with Jaxson—as his fake girlfriend.

Fake girlfriend.

I kept forgetting that.

"Okay, I have shorts. What's next?" I asked, drawing my thoughts from my confusion and focusing on Jaxson.

He studied me, tapping his chin a few times before he nodded. "I'll be right back," he said as he slipped through the bathroom and over to his room.

I hugged the shorts to my chest as I waited. I couldn't imagine what he was getting for me to wear in his room. Whatever it was, I was pretty sure it would look like a potato sack on me.

Or maybe he really thought we wore the same size clothes. Talk about a blow to my self-esteem.

Before I began to spiral, Jaxson appeared, holding his football jersey. The smile on his lips was hard to read, but he looked like Katie on Christmas morning.

Like this was something he'd been waiting to do for a long time.

Which was a ridiculous thought.

"This?" I asked as I took it from him.

A shy expression passed over Jaxson's face as he nodded. "It's what most girlfriends wear. Especially if we're out playing." His grin melted my heart a bit.

Was it wrong that I really liked the fact that he was enjoying this?

Yes. Yes it was. This was fake. For him and for me.

I needed to get that tattooed on my forehead.

"All right," I said as I stepped past him and into the bathroom. Once the door was shut, I slipped out of the banana dress—which I was going to burn later—and into my shorts and his jersey.

I pulled my hair up into a messy bun and tied the bottom of the jersey up so it didn't look like I was wearing a poncho. I took a moment to run my gaze over the front. The team, his number, it was all starting to feel too real.

When I twisted so I could see his last name on the back, my heart took off galloping. It was like he was branding me as his—and that was…confusing.

I swallowed as I pushed out all of my mom's concerns from the other night. I could do this. I was strong.

Wearing his jersey meant nothing.

Nothing.

Not convincing anyone—much less myself—I decided to stop thinking and unlocked the bathroom door. I stepped out as my gaze roamed the room. It took a moment before I located Jaxson. He was standing by my dresser, staring at the picture frames that littered it.

I swallowed as I realized what was still there. My best friends and I from high school. My unruly hair. Braces. It was a time I never wanted Jaxson to remember.

"Those are so old," I said as I rushed over and pushed the picture facedown.

Jaxson chuckled as he turned, and then suddenly he wasn't laughing. Instead, he was staring. At me.

His gaze felt warm as it started on my face and trailed down to the jersey and then my legs. His face flushed again as he cleared his throat and returned his attention to my face.

"You look…my jersey looks good on you," he said as he scrubbed his face.

To say I was nervous was an understatement. The butterflies in my stomach felt as if they had taken up riverdancing. They bounced and jumped all around inside of me.

Before either of us could speak, Liam's voice caused both of us to jump.

"Jaxson? You ready, man?" he asked as his voice grew louder. Suddenly, he appeared in the doorway, and his eyebrows almost disappeared into his hairline. "What are you doing in Lottie's room?" he asked as he folded his arms.

"I was…I mean, she needed…"

"He was just looking at old pictures," I said with a smile and a shrug.

Liam didn't look like he believed me. Instead, he continued to glower at Jaxson. Thankfully, Violet showed up behind him, and when her gaze fell on me she balked.

"She's wearing his jersey. Why can't I wear your jersey?" she asked as she laid her head on Liam's shoulder.

I tried not to vomit as she batted her eyelashes at Liam. I loved my brother, but he stunk at picking girls.

Liam glanced down at her and then sighed as he turned. "Come on, I'll get it for you," he said. And then, just before he disappeared, he threw over his shoulder, "Downstairs in five."

We both nodded, and then the air around Jaxson and I fell silent. I peeked over at him. His expression was hard to read. I swallowed, wondering what he was thinking and what I should say. But, before I could speak, he sighed and made his way to the bathroom.

"See you in five," he said as he shut the door to his room and I was left alone.

Frustrated with my brother, with Jaxson, and with my own lack of ability to succeed at a fake relationship, I busied myself with finding socks and my tennis shoes.

I grabbed my purse and loaded it up with sunscreen and Chapstick. I slung it over my neck as I pulled the door open and stepped out into the hallway. Lucky for me, no one was around. I didn't want to have to make small talk with Jaxson or Violet, and I was getting really tired of the glares Liam cast my direction.

If anything, I needed some Katie love, and, from the sound of the Disney movie that was carrying through the house, I could tell she was home.

I carefully took the stairs one at a time. My ankle was doing so much better, but I wasn't about to tempt fate. I found my niece curled up on the couch, watching the latest release. Her eyes were trained on the screen and her expression was riveted.

She had a bowl of popcorn on her lap and her princess dolls lined up on either side of her.

I smiled as I knelt down in front of her. I reached to take a few pieces of popcorn only to have her swat me away.

"No, Nantie," she said as she pulled the bowl closer to her chest. "Mine."

I feigned a shocked expression and reached over to tousle her hair. Then I turned and pulled my knees up to my chest as I stared at the screen.

I had half a mind to call this whole thing off and just stay home watching movies with Katie. After all, everything here made sense.

And I had become okay with the idea that I was going to be the crazy cat aunt that never got married and lived in her parents' house knitting all day.

Pretending to be the girlfriend of Jaxson the NFL star threw all those plans out the window, and suddenly I didn't know who I was or what I wanted.

Liam, Violet, and Jaxson came down together. They were chatting and laughing like going to a PR photoshoot was as natural as breathing. I watched as they got ready, feeling for the umpteenth time like the little sister tagging along with my big brother and his friends.

They looked so natural. So at home. And I hated that I didn't. I couldn't even figure out what to wear. I'd needed Jaxson's help like I was some child needing help from their parent.

And Violet? She looked so at ease as she flicked her bleach-blonde hair from her shoulder and smiled up at Liam. She had tied his jersey so that her flat, tanned stomach showed above her jeans. Her stiletto heels made her legs look amazing.

I glanced down at my tennis shoes and forced myself not to run upstairs to change. I knew how off-balance I was in heels when I was walking on solid ground. Add grass to the equation and…?

I already had one sore ankle. I didn't need to injure the other one.

We piled into Liam's car. Violet was in the front, and I was in the back with Jaxson. Liam's music made conversation hard as we drove to our alma mater.

Which I was okay with. I really didn't feel like talking, and I most certainly didn't feel like looking over at Jaxson who—from the way he kept glancing in my direction—was desperate to get my attention.

I didn't want to talk to him. I didn't want to talk to anyone. I felt like an outsider looking in, and I feared what Jaxson would say when he realized that he'd made a mistake. That he should have never asked me to be his fake girlfriend.

It was one thing for him to kiss me and forget. It was a whole other thing for him to reject me to my face.

I was strong and resilient, but I was pretty sure a blow like that would end me. There was no way I could come back from something like that.

Call it desperation. Call it my desire to live. Whatever it was, I was going to be the best fake girlfriend a guy could ask for.

I had to be.

10

JAXSON

The old high school field was bright green with neon white lines. They never would have painted those lines in August —school budgets being what they were—unless someone big was coming.

I puffed out my chest, feeling like the big man on campus with the most beautiful girl in school on my arm. Except, Lottie wasn't hanging on my arm like Violet was on Liam. She'd given me the cold shoulder on the ride over, hugging the car door instead of me.

The rebuff was as cold as it was unnecessary. I hadn't crossed any lines. Sure, Liam had been upset that I was in Lottie's room, but it wasn't the first time. Heck, it wasn't even the first time this week. Bro needed to chill.

Yeah, like that was going to happen.

A small crowd of reporters, bloggers, vloggers, and general gawkers had gathered in the stands. Coach Gretzky stood in front of the grass, daring anyone to try and get on his field. The guy's big claim to fame was being second cousins with the famous hockey player. He'd pretty much landed the job based on that, but he'd turned out both Liam and me, so his position was secure until retirement. He was a great coach, tough when he needed to be and just soft enough to be fair when something crappy happened.

Because every season something crappy happened.

During my senior year, our right tackle had broken his arm a week before the first game. He'd come to every practice, but an injury like that didn't allow him to be on the field. Football was this kid's ticket to college because his family was in no position to pay for it.

Coach Gretzky knew this kid had potential, and a scout needed to see it. So, even though Walters hadn't set foot in a game all season, Coach put him in when the college scouts showed up. Last I'd heard, he'd gotten a degree and worked as an engineer at a company designing computer chips for cell phones in Japan.

These were the kind of men who made this sport great in my eyes. So, when Coach stuck out his hand, I went in for a bear hug. Coach grunted on impact and slammed me on the back repeatedly.

The cameras loved it, but I didn't give a rip about that. When I let him go, Coach cleared his throat and looked away for a minute. When he turned back, his hard-nosed game face was in place. "Get on the field!" he barked.

"Yes, sir!" Liam and I grinned. A spike of adrenaline shot through me—a Pavlovian response to hearing the command. I grabbed Lottie's hand and tugged her onto the grass, unwilling to let her get too far away. If she'd loosen up, this would be a lot of fun.

Violet squealed behind us.

Lottie laughed quietly. "Her heels are sinking in the grass."

I grinned down at her. "Coach won't appreciate her version of aerating the field."

We watched as Liam found a spot for Violet on the bench before running out to join us.

"Is Violet not coming?" I feigned concern. It wasn't the first time I'd had to pretend to care that the overrated prima donna wasn't along for the fun, and I thought I had the routine down.

Lottie elbowed me in the stomach. She saw right through my facade. Thankfully, Liam was already sizing up the seniors on the field and missed it. I squeezed her side in retaliation and she jolted at my touch.

For a moment, I wondered if it was me. If she could feel the lightning between us; or if she was just that ticklish. Using a lighter touch, I tried to tickle her again, but she sidestepped me. I narrowed my eyes. "You know, a player only gets away from me once."

Her eyes sparkled with mischief, and my heart dropped to the ground and then bounced up to the sky. "We'll see about that."

"Game on." I laced my fingers together and stretched my arms above my head. I was so winning this.

Liam welcomed the kids out for the day and thanked them for coming. The team captain, Kayden, stepped forward and shook hands all around. Lottie giggled at his seriousness. "I totally babysat him."

I chuckled. "Lucky kid," I muttered under my breath. Having Lottie all to myself for an afternoon sounded like a lot of fun. There would be serious tickle challenges that ended in fits of laughter and maybe even…I cut those thoughts out of my head like my mom clipping coupons. No way could I go there. Lottie was already on my mind way too often. If I started thinking about holding her close, I'd never come back to real life.

She leaned over a little and whispered, "He used to eat glue."

I burst out a laugh at her memory of the team captain. Thank goodness my babysitters weren't here today.

Liam glared over his shoulder at the two of us like an annoyed mother telling her kids to zip it.

"Okay, so we're going to have you guys throw for us, and we'll walk around and talk to each of you. Then we'll do some drills. Grab a partner." Liam reached into the rolling container of footballs and threw one to Kayden, who caught the ball and grabbed the kid next to him and trotted down the field to line up.

Lottie shook out her hands.

"You okay?" I asked.

She nodded. "I was pretty nervous coming. I mean, this is not my scene." She gestured to the cameras and fans.

I faltered. Lottie always seemed to know just who she was and that was downright attractive in a woman.

"But I'm feeling a little better. I mean, as long as I don't have to talk to a bunch of reporters, I should be good." She wiped her palms on her cutoff shorts. Those legs. Geez. How was a guy supposed to concentrate?

What were we talking about?

A ball flew at Lottie's face. Her hands flew up protectively, and she ducked. I instinctively grabbed for it. "Liam!" she scolded.

Liam smirked. "You two need to keep your eye on the ball." He gave me a hard look.

I felt the warning all the way to my shoes. I was getting too comfortable with Liam's little sister—even though we were essentially in a fishbowl and every look, every touch was being recorded.

I tossed the ball to her. "I'm going to talk to some of the guys. Do you, uh, want to sit with Violet?" A little distance was just what the older brother ordered.

She snorted and then her cheeks burned red. I loved that this was her response to me. She didn't blush when her brothers teased her, but she did it all the time around me. Like when she'd said she looked like a banana in the yellow dress. She hadn't, she'd looked good—but she looked better in my jersey.

"I'd rather not."

I hooked my arm around her waist, laying my hand flat so she didn't think I was going to tickle her. I didn't want her dancing out of my hold, because she fit perfectly right where she was. "Can we just agree that Violet is the worst girlfriend he could have picked." I led her to the opposite side of the field from Liam. I wouldn't forget that the dude was there and do something crazy, but I was tired of being chastised for enjoying Lottie's company.

After all, we were fake-dating. That had to give me some leeway.

"Thank you!" She relaxed against me. "I don't want to say anything bad about her—I mean, she's…"

"Yep, she is that." I pulled her close for a hug of sorts and then let go. Holding her like that was doing funny things to my mind. Like making me forget we were in front of the cameras. Or that there were a bunch of teenagers dying for five minutes of my time.

I did my best to focus on the first set of kids, but my eyes were constantly drawn back to Lottie.

She had a cute little nose that turned up slightly at the end. And where did those freckles come from? Had they always been there?

"He's rotating his shoulder too much." She nodded to the guy on our right, number 67.

I pulled my attention away from her and watched 67 throw. Sure enough, he twisted too much when he threw. He was losing power. I stared at her, my mouth hanging open. "How did you see that?"

She shrugged. "You think you're the only one who watched those training videos?"

I flashed back to the afternoons Liam and I spent in their home theater, watching YouTube videos from the pros and the guys who trained the pros. We'd even convinced his dad to shell out $500 for the complete set. A vague memory of Lottie coming in with a bowl of popcorn surfaced. "You make great popcorn." I smiled.

She flipped her ponytail over her shoulder and gave me a sultry look. "Oh, I know how to work a microwave."

Could this woman be any hotter?

"Jaxson," called one of the kids.

I did my best to ignore the slow burn starting in my chest and looked over at number 54. "Yeah?"

"How far can you throw?" He had a cocky tip to his head and a swagger that was too big for his britches. He was out to challenge the big dogs.

I grinned, took the ball from Lottie and threw it right between the two goalposts on the other end of the field. A kid let out a whistle, and 54's buddy shoved him.

"Now go get it, 54," barked Coach.

Lottie shook her head. "Boys."

We ran through drills. Nothing that would work up too much of a sweat for me or Liam because we were here to get good pics as well as help the kids. But the players were in full uniform, and they left dripping.

We shook hands with Coach as the boys headed for the showers, thanking him for the opportunity to come back to our old haunt. It was a strange thing to be saying goodbye once again.

Violet grabbed onto Liam's arm and snuggled up against him. "You looked so good out there, babe."

I perked up. I was ready for Lottie to throw a compliment my way. I'd told her she looked good in my jersey, but she hadn't reciprocated. Instead, Lottie made a small, almost indiscernible gagging noise.

"Don't you think you should be talking up my game?" I prodded. "It's what a girlfriend does."

"Fake girlfriend," she said only loud enough for the two of us to hear.

I didn't like the reminder. It sat on my conscience like a fumble on the second yard line. Like this wasn't how it was supposed to go down.

The closer we got to the reporters, the more I had to drag her along. Her eyes were wide with fear. I hated making her go over there, but this was part of the deal. Still... "If you want to cut out right now, we can hide in the tunnel." I nodded to the gaping hole the players had trudged through to get to the locker rooms.

She pressed her lips tight and shook her head. "I can do this."

I nodded and caught her eye, wishing I could hand her a bunch of my experience and calm. "I know you can."

She seemed to drink in my confidence and her steps lengthened.

"I'll be right here the whole time." I drew her closer to me, thinking I could shield her from all this.

When we were five feet away, the questions started. The energy was equivalent to throwing a hot dog in the middle of the pound. I was used to it—had managed the chaos hundreds of times. But I could feel Lottie shrinking into herself, and the sensation made my heart clinch.

"Lottie, Jaxson—tell us how you met!"

She moved almost behind me.

I glanced down at her and then at Liam.

Liam held up a hand to draw attention. "I introduced them—in a way. Jaxson is my buddy and Lottie's my little sister."

A puff of disgust escaped Lottie's lips. I rolled over Liam's answer and realized she didn't like being called "little sister." I tucked the information away to ponder later. She did step partially out from behind me, though, asserting herself. Hmm. Interesting.

"Did you two date in high school?"

Considering her reaction to being called the little sister, I felt like I should tread lightly here. "She was way out of my league."

That earned me some chuckles and a grateful look from Lottie.

"How about a kiss for the camera?" An overly eager woman with a ponytail that bounced when she talked, smiled gleefully.

Liam didn't skip a beat. "Sure." He dipped Violet and kissed her good.

Violet made little hms and moans that made me want to gag.

Lottie wrinkled her nose. I was able to keep my expression neutral. But only because I'd had years of training. Liam wasn't known around town as a shy guy—especially when he had a woman on his arm.

When Liam brought Violet back up to standing, she carefully checked her hair and lipstick. Not one camera had clicked during their display.

An uncomfortable silence hung over the crowd of reporters as they waited to see who would point out the obvious fact that they had meant me and Lottie.

"You're turn," said a perky brunette as she lifted her camera, pointing it at me.

I heard Liam growl, but I chose to ignore it. We were fake-dating. He had to know kissing came with the territory.

The only person I was going to pay attention to was Lottie. I glanced at her, waiting for permission. She smiled, though her eyes were everywhere but on me. That just wouldn't do. No matter how hard my pulse pounded in my ears, blocking out all the calls for us to kiss that only increased in volume. And no matter how much I wanted to taste those strawberry lips, I would not force this upon her. I tickled her side, lightly enough that she wouldn't jump, and whispered in her ear. "You don't have to."

She turned, our faces only a deep breath apart, and searched my eyes. The moment stretched on as she traced my cheek. "It's just a kiss."

It wasn't quite the permission I wanted, but I wasn't going to stand around like an idiot anymore. If Lottie saw this as *just* a kiss, I was going to show her what *just* a kiss was. Slowly, I lowered my lips to hers. She was warm and soft, familiar.

Suddenly, my mind opened up a memory, one I'd tucked away years ago for my own survival.

I'd kissed Lottie before.

I stilled, the memory of that sweet kiss on graduation night and this one blending together to forever brand me as hers.

"*B*ut, it is a big deal. It's my first kiss."

I heard Lottie's voice through the decorations and the trees in her backyard but couldn't see her. If there was some guy out here, trying to talk her into kissing, he had another thing coming. No one messed with Lottie.

The McKnights had put together an epic graduation party for me and Liam. I was flying high, on scholarship, feeling like the king of the world, and I'd called my dad to rub it in. To show him that I'd succeeded in spite of him leaving me behind. Only, Dad hadn't been impressed. He'd said I was selfish and too young to know what success really was. He'd told me to grow up.

So I hadn't felt like jumping back into the party and had wandered out of sight.

Curiosity won out, and I moved to hide in the back where the shadows were deep and long. I walked around the fountain/planter thingy and listened to see if I needed to pound some guy for getting handsy with my best friend's sister.

"So I just...lean?" Lottie was talking to Sarah, not a guy. My heart rate went down a notch.

"Yeah. And he'll do the rest." Sarah snapped her gum. "I'll go find him.

You wait here." She bounded away like an energizer bunny hyped up on Kool-Aid.

"But..." Lottie wrung her hands.

I smiled, bemused. It was sweet, really. The way she was stressed about kissing a guy. The least I could do was help put her mind at ease. We men weren't all that complicated. I stepped out of my hiding spot and into view, my feet loud on the pea gravel.

Lottie whipped around, and her face instantly turned tomato red.

"I, uh, couldn't help but overhear." I nodded in the direction Sarah had bounded off. "She's right, you know. It's not that big of a deal. It's just kissing."

"Kill me now." Lottie turned away from me.

I frowned. First my dad treated me like nothing, and now she acted like I had no idea what I was talking about. Well, I'd show her. I closed the distance between us, took her arm and spun her around, letting her body land against mine. She was soft and curvy in the right places.

She gasped, her hands going to my chest.

"I'll bet you're better at kissing than you think," I said before I pressed my lips to hers.

Lottie melted.

I'd never had a girl lean in so fully or give me such control over her lips. It confused and excited me. Even though Dad thought I was a failure at everything, Lottie trusted me. I threaded my fingers into her hair and cupped the back of her head.

Footsteps sounded close, and I stepped back, making sure she was solid on her feet. We looked at one another for a moment, and then I heard Liam call my name. Reality hit.

I'd crossed a line.

Big time.

A tug on my arm brought me back to the present. I pulled back from the kiss and stared down, half expecting to see the younger Lottie in my arms. When our foreheads touched, her eyes were luminous, and her deep breaths matched the tempo of my own. I swallowed.

Kissing grown-up Lottie had scrambled my brain cells. And then there was the graduation kiss. Had it really been her first one? I hoped so.

How could I have forgotten? Did Lottie remember?

She'd never mentioned it. Maybe she was waiting for me to say something. Why hadn't I said something? That whole evening had been a blur. I'd made a lot of mistakes that night, and kissing Lottie was one of them. But I'd been desperate. Anything to take away the sting of Dad's rebuff.

And maybe, I was protecting myself. If I admitted to myself and to Liam what I'd done, I'd only make my father's words come true. It was a confusing and frustrating time. And I'd dragged Lottie into the middle of it. Only a jerk would kiss Lottie and then never speak about it again.

And only an idiot would forget that kiss completely.

"When did you realize you were in love?" called a reporter.

"Just this moment," I said without thinking. I received another poke in my back that was decidedly Liam-like. And it was harder than the last one. "Just like every moment when we kiss—she takes my breath away."

Thankfully, Liam wrapped up the interview and ushered us all to the car. With the way I was feeling, I feared what I might accidently say.

Violet pouted and ducked into her seat. I was about to follow Lottie into the backseat when Liam grabbed my arm and pulled me a few feet away, shutting the door on Lottie.

"Can you not grope my sister?" he growled.

I glanced at him and held my breath for a moment. I needed to keep my cool. If Liam got even an inkling that I had feelings for his sister, I was in trouble. "It was for the camera. It wasn't like I could say no."

Liam stared off at the field. "It looked real, man. And you're not that good of an actor. What the heck?"

"Maybe I…" I almost let it slip. My confusing feelings that, maybe, it was more than just a kiss. But I stopped myself. Liam was an understanding guy when it came to a lot of things. But when it came to matters of the heart? Especially when it included his sister. He wasn't going to care how I felt.

"You agreed. My sister is off-limits. Do your publicity stunt, but don't drag her into this world. She's too sweet. Too innocent for you, man." He stormed back to the car.

I stood there for a moment, my gaze trained on the football field, but I wasn't really looking. Instead I was thinking about Lottie and how it felt to have her pressed against me. That mixed with my friendship with Liam and his reaction toward our kiss.

And suddenly, this super simple arrangement didn't feel so simple anymore. I'd thought I could handle my feelings, but I was beginning to think I'd overestimated myself.

There was a small possibility that what Liam said about me was right, but when it came to Lottie, he was wrong. She wasn't this innocent little sister anymore. There was a side to her. One I was pretty sure Liam had never seen.

But I felt it when I laughed with her—when I looked at her. Lottie was a woman. Mysterious and confusing. I was drawn to her. I wanted to learn more about her.

Even it if meant going behind my best friend's back, I couldn't help it.

Lottie had changed me, and I wasn't about to walk away.

Not yet.

11

LOTTIE

I'd never been more confused than the day after I kissed Jaxson—the second time.

Even the first kiss hadn't been this mixed up. I mean, it didn't take me long to understand that he'd been trying to show me that a kiss wasn't a big deal—to him. To me it had been huge. Still was, if I was honest with myself. Which, let's face it, it was so much more fun to lie to myself and think that he'd felt something, that I wasn't the only one who'd had a profound shift in those few seconds our lips were pressed together.

But I couldn't afford to lie to myself about this kiss.

This one had moved me.

And created questions. So many questions.

How was I supposed to hold all my feelings for him back when Jaxson was such a good kisser? And that look he'd given me right after? The one that said he was looking into my soul in a way no man had before—that he saw me? That had me discombobulated.

My morning was a mess. Katie was patient with me—thank goodness. When I forgot the milk in her cereal, she said, "Nantie—need moo moo!"

And, when I stared at the remote control instead of pushing play, she about tugged my arm out of the socket. "Nantie. Stristoff." The little munchkin had a thing for Kristoff. I couldn't blame her—he was the kind of true-blue, brave cutie we should all be lucky enough to find.

Kristoff came back for true love's kiss—he hadn't run away from it.

I was so tangled up in my own head that when Suzie called and demanded we hang out, I agreed in a Peloponnesian minute.

Maybe she'd have better relationship advice than a cartoon princess.

She picked up Chinese food, powdered doughnuts, and sparkling water on her way over, which made her the best friend in existence. There was nothing like fried rice and orange chicken to drown my worries.

Katie wanted to go swimming, so Suzie borrowed a suit and we proceeded to set up a picnic under the poolside umbrella in the backyard.

The pool area was fenced in. Mom had shrubs planted to hide the black iron fence around the deep end. There was another entrance to the pool over there. We used it when people came for swim parties because they could go right out to their cars and not track water through the house.

Katie set up her own girl talk spot with her Barbies on the swim deck and left me and Suzie to our own devices. The sun was only interrupted by a few cute clouds now and then. With everyone out of the house and the television off, I finally started to relax.

We were munching on egg rolls and watching Katie splash in the water while I updated Suzie on the whole Jaxson situation and the fake-date the day before. Jaxson and I had agreed that only family would know that the relationship wasn't real, but Suzie was family to me. She'd been around since we were both in diapers, so that qualified her to know my deepest secrets.

Suzie's mouth dropped more and more as I talked. Considering my history of not getting anywhere with Jaxson, I could understand her shock that we'd gone from I don't know you're alive to kissing in front of the whole world.

"Your life is so great right now. If I didn't love you to pieces, I'd hate your guts." She took a swig of her drink.

I picked at the flaky roll, keeping my gaze downturned. "Great? Did you not hear anything I just said?"

Suzie snorted. "Girl, you're fake-dating an NFL player. Your face has literally become a meme." She lifted her phone and, a few seconds later, shoved the screen under my nose.

There was a picture of Jaxson and me, lip-locked. "Scores Touchdowns and the Women" was written across the top and bottom. I grabbed her phone. My cheeks felt like I'd forgotten SPF 30 and landed on the sun.

"Oh my gosh," I said as I shoved the remaining egg roll into my mouth. "Social media sucks."

Suzie laughed as she grabbed a fortune cookie and opened the plastic. "You're living the life most women dream of. You're bound to get haters."

I swallowed, the edges of the egg roll scraping my throat as it went down. The truth was, Suzie was wrong. I wasn't living a life. I wasn't...anything. I wasn't Jaxson's girlfriend. I wasn't his fling. I wasn't even his friend.

After we got back from the high school, he'd packed up his duffle bag and escaped to the gym. Penny needed to work that night, so I'd watched Katie. Even after watching Frozen two times, Jaxson hadn't returned.

I went to bed singing "Let It Go" to myself and dreamed of Jaxson riding in on a reindeer and whisking me away to his ice castle.

Even this morning, he was nowhere to be found. I may have snuck into his room to see if he was there. You know, because I have a responsibility as his fake girlfriend to see that he's alive every now and again. His bed was made and his room disappointedly empty.

We'd made some headway as friends, at least I thought we had. But it appeared that I'd gone from sort of talking to Jaxson to chasing him off.

And there was a part of me that feared it was because of our kiss. He'd done it before. Kissed me and run away.

Maybe this was a thing.

Maybe I sucked at kissing. No pun intended.

No. Pun intended. I thought back to the kiss to try to remember if I'd sucked his lip into my mouth accidentally. No kissing faux pas stuck out in my memory. And no other guy I'd kissed had ever complained.

I swallowed as I forced myself to stop overthinking. I was beginning to spiral—I could feel it.

"This whole thing is just a big, colossal mess," I said as I pushed my plate away and rested my forehead on my arms. "I'm calling it off." This was why I shouldn't have agreed to date Jaxson, fake or otherwise. My emotions were too close to the surface to really shove them down where they needed to be in order to survive.

Suzie tapped my head. "Are you crazy?" she asked, her voice rising an octave.

I raised my gaze to meet hers and glared. "Pretty much?"

She stared at me. "Did you not hear me say that *you're living the life most women dream of?*"

I sighed and pushed off the table. My shoulders were hunched, and my back curved forward. I'm sure I looked like the poster child for confidence.

"Feeling confused and reading into everything is what women dream of?" I pulled the bag of powdered sugar doughnuts my direction and took one out, shoving the whole thing in my mouth. Self-medicating with sugar was a great coping skill. "I'm the unemployed fake girlfriend to a guy who disappears after he kisses me." Sugar flew from my lips as I spoke, but I didn't care. I was wallowing and I was good at it. "Some role model."

Suzie sighed as she looked at me like I had two heads. "You get to kiss, touch, and flirt with a hot guy. No strings attached. Not just any hot guy but *the* hot guy that you've been fantasizing about since high school. On top of that, he's rich and famous, so he can take you to

94

fancy places and buy you things." She rolled her eyes. "It's like the *Crazy Rich Asians* movement completely missed you."

Now she was talking gibberish. "The what now?" I asked as I licked the remaining sugar from my fingers.

Suzie waved her hand. "*Crazy Rich Asians*? The movie? An unsuspecting girl falls for a rich man." She waved her hand toward me and then toward the house—which I assumed meant that she was gesturing toward Jaxson.

"Like *Pretty Woman*?" I asked, fishing out another doughnut. My mom used to love that show, and we both grew up watching it with her.

Suzie slapped the table with her hands. "Exactly...well, except for the whole prostitute thing."

I snorted as I picked off a bit of doughnut and slipped it into my mouth. My thoughts went to Liam and what he would do if he heard this conversation. I was pretty sure the words "manslaughter" and "ten feet under" would be thrown around. He didn't like me kissing Jaxson in front of people, and he certainly wouldn't like me playing it *just for fun*. The echo of the car door slamming in my face yesterday still rang through my head. Neither of them told me what they had talked about, but I had a pretty good idea.

I cleared my throat as I adjusted my legs to stretch them out in front of me. "So what you're saying"—I narrowed my eyes in her direction—"is that I should keep fake-dating him so he'll buy me pretty things?"

"Of course. Use this to your advantage. You're helping him out and suffering for it. You should be compensated by a little something on the side."

I blinked a few times. I had not expected her to say that. Especially not in that way. "I'm already getting something, an in with the team. I don't feel bad about that, because it won't cost him a dime. If I start demanding jewelry, won't that be using him? Or extortion or something?"

"Okay, forget the jewelry. But go for the cuddles." She winked. "He's so cuddly."

I laughed.

He was hot. He was sweet. And his kiss turned my knees to Jell-O. I'd enjoyed wrapping my arms around him and holding him close. It was what happened after that wasn't any fun—the worrying over it. What if I just let go of that worry? What if I could be in the moment and not stress over the next?

What was wrong with having a little fun?

And then a little tug pulled at the back of my mind. I knew why I was hesitant. I knew why this was different for me than it would be for any other girl.

It wasn't just some billionaire in a screenplay. This was Jaxson I was thinking about.

Jaxson.

And he wasn't just some guy. At least, not to me.

So I sighed as I crossed my arms in front of my chest. Maybe I felt crossing them would protect me. Protect my heart.

"I don't think I can do that," I said, my voice turning to a whisper.

Suzie watched me with a sympathetic expression. She leaned over and patted my arm. "Just try. For me, for the rest of the women on the planet who would give our first-born child for this opportunity. Just one more shot. You never know. Maybe this is the kind of fun you need to have. Then you'll know when a relationship is right. When it's the one."

She shrugged. "What's that saying? You can't know the sweet until you know the bitter. Why wouldn't that apply to your situation?" She swung her legs over the bench and stood. After slipping off her swimsuit cover, she glanced over at me. "You deserve to have fun. Lots. Just think about it."

I nodded to appease her as she turned and sprinted to the deep end of the pool. After cannonballing into the water, she swam over to Katie, who was diving a doll through the water like a mermaid.

I watched them play for a few minutes, trying to wrap my mind around what Suzie had said. I wanted to believe that I was a "do it 'cause I deserve it" kind of girl, but I wasn't so sure.

Something had changed over the past couple of days. The same thing had happened back in high school when Jaxson kissed me at his graduation party. Suddenly, the thing that was holding me to the ground wasn't gravity...but him.

I couldn't 100% fake a relationship with him. There was always going to be a part of me that wished for something more. The real question was, could I ignore that voice enough to keep up this charade?

I stood and stretched. If I wanted to survive the next few weeks with Jaxson, I needed to stop thinking. Stress was the last thing I needed. If anything, it was just going to confuse me more.

Right now, feeling the cool pool water on my skin and laughing with Suzie and Katie sounded like the perfect way to decompress. Plus, I'd pounded down some major caloric therapy and could use a swim.

I pulled off my cover, revealing my black one-piece. It was simple but elegant. There was this lacy detail around the middle that exposed my midriff just right while still giving a hint of mystery.

I wasn't a two-piece kind of gal. Call me crazy, but I liked the idea of a guy guessing about the goods underneath.

I made my way to the deep end to jump. Just as I passed by the diving board, two hands grabbed my waist, stopping me from leaping into the pool.

I screamed and wiggled around to see Jaxson's amused expression. He must have come through the driveway entrance. Before I could get my bearings and scold him, he pulled me closer. There was a hint of mystery in his eyes, and his gaze swept over me.

"What are you doing?" I finally breathed out. I was trying—and failing—to ignore the feel of his arm wrapped around my waist. And the fact that he seemed to lean further into me with every passing second.

My hands warmed as they were sprawled out on his biceps. His huge, even for him, muscles were like the sun. Hot to touch and physically impossible to ignore.

"I've been looking all over for you," he said. His voice was gruff as he stared at me.

And I mean *stared*. There was this intensity to his gaze. Like, out of everything in this world that he could look at, all he wanted to focus on was me.

It made the butterflies in my stomach take off. If I could have stepped back, I would have. But the only place to go was the pool, and I wasn't ready to leave quite yet.

"Well, I've been here. Last night and all of today," I said sarcastically. I clamped my lips shut. I didn't want to sound like an ignored girlfriend begging for attention. I was independent and confident—a woman all my own. It wasn't like I was sitting around waiting for him to grace me with his presence. Ugh!

He must have picked up on the sarcasm in my voice because his brow furrowed and he tipped his head to the side. Then he blinked and straightened. "I was wondering if I could call in a favor, fake girlfriend."

I know he was trying to flirt—trying to make this awkward situation less awkward—but hearing the words "fake girlfriend" was like a dagger to my heart.

I didn't want him to feel bad, and I most certainly didn't want him to know how I felt about him. That was a secret I was going to keep in the Vault-o-Lottie.

So I gave him my most flirty smile—I hoped—and I shrugged. "What do you need me for?"

He stepped back and pushed his hands through his hair. He glanced at me and then quickly looked away, and I got the feeling that he hadn't meant to hold me for so long.

What was that about?

"I was hoping you'd come be a hero for some sick kids."

I studied him, trying to figure out what he was talking about. "I'm sorry, what?"

"She'll do it if you buy her a necklace," Suzie said from the pool.

I shot Jaxson an apologetic smile. "She's joking."

Jaxson looked amused as he glanced from me to Suzie. "Are you her agent now?" he asked.

Suzie must have moved through the water like a dolphin to get over here without me hearing her splash. That, or I'd been so wrapped up in being in Jaxson's arms that the whole world had disappeared.

Suzie clung to the edge of the pool, her gaze fixed on Jaxson. "I'm just looking out for her. You know, making sure she gets a fair trade."

I heard Jaxson's soft chuckle as he nodded and then slipped his gaze over to me. "I'll buy you whatever you want," he said. There was a depth to his voice that sent shivers down my back.

I swallowed and, when that didn't move the emotions that were lodged in my throat, I coughed. "It's fine. You don't have to pay me. I'm good with the recommendation to the team."

Jaxson shook his head as he stepped forward. "I want to." He was inches away now. I could feel his warmth cascading all over me. His gaze was trained on my face, and his lips parted as his eyes dropped to my clavicle. He reached up and brushed his fingers against my skin. "It'd be a shame to leave this kind of real estate bare."

His fingers lingered for a moment before he blinked and stepped back. He shoved his hands into the front pockets of his jeans and squinted as he glanced over to the house. "We're leaving in fifteen." Then his glanced back at me, his gaze roaming over my body. A smile twitched at his lips as he met my gaze. "You might want to change."

Feeling like a complete idiot, standing there in a bathing suit while he was nicely clad in jeans and a polo shirt, I nodded. "Right. Yeah. I'll change." I took a few steps back.

He nodded and lifted his hand in Suzie's direction. "Always good to see you again, Suz," he said. Then he glanced back over at me. "I'll leave your outfit on your bed."

I parted my lips to ask for more details, but he didn't wait. Instead, he turned and, a few seconds later, was gone.

When he disappeared from view, I let out my breath as I slumped against the diving board's stairs. I blinked a few times and then glanced over at Suzie. She was amused by our interaction and doing nothing to hide it.

Realizing that I'd just agreed to leave when I was supposed to be watching Katie, I straightened. "I'm the worst aunt ever. I can't go with Jaxson." I groaned as I tipped my head back.

"Well, it's a good thing I'm here with absolutely nothing to do." She waved her arms back and forth as she tread water.

I peeked over at my friend. "You're okay with that?"

Suzie snorted. "Of course. After all, I'm determined to help you get out of this funk. You're either going to fall in love with Jaxson or finally get over him." She flipped onto her back. "Either way, you'll finally figure out your crap."

I nodded as I twisted my hair around my finger. My nerves were bundled as I stared off toward the house.

"Plus, if he picks me up a little something as a thank you gift, I wouldn't object." Suzie's voice broke through my thoughts.

I shot her a look and she laughed.

"What's with you and getting gifts?" I asked as I wandered over to my swimsuit cover and slipped it on.

"Let's just say I'm a take-advantage-of-the-situation kind of gal," she called after me.

I'd slipped on my flip-flops and started speed walking to the house. "Of course you are," I threw over my shoulder. "Take care of Katie, I'll be back later," I said as I slid open the glass door and entered the air-conditioned house.

I took a deep breath as I hurried across the carpet and up the stairs to my room. My nerves fired as I tried to analyze what we were going to do. Where Jaxson was going to take me.

Whatever it was, one thing was for sure, I was excited to spend more time with Jaxson. And suddenly, my desire to call things off vanished into thin air.

I closed my door and leaned against the frame as I blew out my breath. I needed to get a grip. This was just a fake date—er, excursion.

It meant nothing.

Right?

12

JAXSON

*W*e had to enter the hospital through the women's center. Construction was all over the parking lot and part of the hospital. They were expanding. No wonder the mayor wanted this year's fundraiser to be the biggest ever.

My face itched so bad I wanted to Hulk out and rip at the tattered tee shirt stretched across my chest. The thick layer of green paint sounded like a good idea when I'd seen the costume at the local party shop. But it was quickly proving to be horrible.

I might have an allergy.

No matter how uncomfortable I was, I was not going to back out on these kids.

When Brent had called to set up the visit, the volunteer coordinator gently mentioned that the younger kids liked superheroes. I was not offended, though I think Brent was. He had this idea that my face was my brand and it needed to be everywhere. I think he was even working on a lunch box deal.

I assured him I was willing to wear a mask and still post pictures. Besides, for me it wasn't about the social-media hype or gaining a thousand new followers. It was about the kids.

But I'm not gonna lie. Lottie looked darn good as Wonder Woman.

That girl had legs. Long and practically perfect. Gone were the knobby knees of a teenager. She was irresistible now.

When I'd seen her poolside, I'd had to rein in my manly instinct to throw her over my shoulder and haul her off to my cave.

Me Jaxson.

Me idiot.

And then when she came down the stairs in the Wonder Woman costume I'd picked out for her, I had half a mind to call this whole thing off. It was one thing to have me covered in green paint, it was a whole other thing to parade Lottie around where there were other men with eyes. Looking at her.

My skin heated as I swallowed down the anger that boiled up at the mere thought of someone else looking at her.

I was the idiot who couldn't seem to get it through my head that Lottie wasn't mine. We weren't really dating. I had no right to try and protect her like that. If she wanted to date some hoity-toity doctor, who was I to stop her?

"Dumb doctor," I muttered under my breath as we walked next to each other.

Lottie didn't seem to notice my momentary freak out as she cautiously tugged at the top of her costume. Thankfully, it came up high enough that she wasn't giving away any secrets.

"You look great." I smiled at her, wondering if the effect was ruined by the green makeup. It had gone on thick, and I wasn't sure I got it everywhere.

"I feel like I'm walking around in my swimsuit." She shot me a dirty look.

"Do you wear boots in the pool?"

"No." She looked down her nose at me.

The boots were one of my favorite parts of the costume. Red and gold, they came up over her knees and had a two-inch heel. I looked down to take them in and ran into a gurney someone had left in the hallway.

Lottie snickered. "You might have to jump in the pool to get all that makeup off."

I rolled my eyes. "I'll be cleaning it out of my ears for weeks." I made my hands into fists to keep from rubbing at the itching spots.

Lottie laughed, and suddenly it didn't seem so bad.

We rounded the corner to the children's wing and met up with Ashley Turnbow, the assistant volunteer coordinator over the children's cancer floor. She was Asian, with short-cropped black hair and an infectious smile.

"Jaxson, it's so good to meet you." She thrust out her hand.

I shook it. "This is my…" I caught on the word for just a moment but recovered quickly, "girlfriend, Lottie. Charlotte." I looked at Lottie, wondering how she'd want me to introduce her.

She shook Ashely's hand. "Lottie's fine."

"Great. Great. Well, thanks for going all out on the costumes. The kids are going to flip. I hope you aren't too upset about it?" She gave one of those smiles that was both apologetic and glad that she'd got what she wanted.

"Anything we can do to make this day better for these kids," I said.

"You really are a hero." She patted my arm.

"I'm not." I glanced at Lottie, wondering if she thought I was a hero too. I didn't bring her to show off, but I wouldn't mind making a good impression. I wanted her to see me as the guy she made me feel like when we'd kissed. The one who was, well, amazing.

"He's not," Lottie said in all seriousness. "He's just a regular guy who leaves his dishes in the sink."

My face heated to the point where I felt the makeup soften. "I do not."

She laughed easily, her head tipping back a little and her eyes dancing. She'd gotten me.

"No one gets me twice." I shook a finger at her.

"This way." Smiling at our banter, Ashley led us down the sterile hall. The walls had framed pictures made out of handprints in primary colors. There was a turkey with the beak painted on the thumb, an apple tree, and even a porcupine.

We passed a doctor, his lab coat as white as snow. He'd been looking down at a chart but glanced up when Ashley said hello. His eyes darted to Lottie and then widened. I'd seen that look many times on a man's face, and I didn't appreciate it being aimed at my girlfriend —even if our relationship was fake. I took her hand and gave the guy an "off-limits" glare.

Lottie lifted our joined hands and then lifted an eyebrow, questioning my PDA.

I shrugged. She could think it was to keep up appearances, and not to chase off every male within thirty miles.

"A hospital is a tight community, as you know," Lottie said.

"Of course." I hoped so. Let that guy tell all his little doctor friends that Wonder Woman was taken.

"So, Carter and Penny are going to hear about this." She swung our hands back and forth.

I lowered my voice and leaned in. "That's the idea, right? We want people to think we're dating."

She pressed her lips together for a moment. I could see her thoughts spinning in her mind. Then whatever was holding her back faded and her expression cleared. "You're right. Let's give them something to talk about." She winked.

Was she serious? The implications of that statement ran through my mind faster than the play called on the field.

I brushed my thumb over her knuckles, enjoying the feel of her soft skin. But I didn't have a lot of time to explore the sensations it created inside of me, because we'd made it to the patients' rooms.

Inside the first door, a small boy was sitting cross-legged on his bed, playing a video game. He paused it when Ashely walked in, and his mouth dropped open when me and Lottie followed.

"Oh my gosh!" He got on his knees on the bed. "Hulk smash!" He started hitting his pillows with his fists and then threw them off the bed.

Usually when I did these visits, I was me. Kids wanted an autographed ball or to measure my biceps. But I loved his enthusiasm, so I jumped right in with him. "Smash," I yelled, lowering my voice and clomping over to the bed. I raised my fists and then brought my arms down, flexing like a professional wrestler, and growled. The kid did the same.

Lottie chortled behind me.

Yeah, I was pretty much being an idiot. But could she see this kid's face? I turned to gauge her reaction and found her standing with her fists on her hips and her feet spread apart in the perfect Wonder Woman pose. She even had the regal lift to her chin like Diana.

"Hulk," she said in censure, "we don't smash the hospital."

I exaggerated my deflating. "Hulk sorry."

"It's okay, big guy." She patted my back as she walked toward the bed and eyed our little Hulk wannabe. She'd even done an accent that was spot on. "We're looking for heroes. Think you can help us out?"

"Yes! Yes!" His eyes shone so bright.

Lottie held out a hand. "Let's see if you're tall enough. Stand up."

He nodded and worked his way to his feet. He was a little wobbly, so she steadied him as she looked him up and down. I went over and did the same, putting my face right next to his head and sniffing like a puppy. He giggled.

"What's your name?" Lottie asked.

"Trevor." He patted my head. My hair was sprayed green and wouldn't move in a tornado. He wrinkled his nose. I mirrored his expression.

"Trevor, do you swear to fight for justice? To only 'smash' when you're defending truth and right?"

"I swear," he repeated with all the vehemence in his body.

"Then I officially welcome you into the club." She hugged him and he hugged her back.

Lucky kid. His brown eyes met mine, expecting something. So far, I'd been a great prop. I needed to up my game. "Hulk proud." I pounded my fist against my chest. Trevor giggled.

We talked for a few more minutes about his video game while staying in character which meant I could only put three words together. Lottie asked great questions, and I gave silly answers.

Ashley had a Polaroid camera, and she took a picture of the three of us, handing Trevor the print as soon as it came out. "Don't touch it until the picture has a chance to appear, okay?"

He nodded. "I won't. My dad has a camera like that. He takes pictures of us all the time."

"Sweet." Lottie leaned over and kissed his hair. She closed her eyes, and I could see compassion flood her face. She'd done so well keeping her emotions in check so Trevor wouldn't notice her heart aching for him. His inner light was so bright it could have powered the hospital.

My heart constricted at the sight of Lottie's pain, and a protective side of me rose up. It was that same feeling I'd had when I kissed her years ago—she made me better.

As we left the room, I put my arm around her. "I'm sorry. I didn't mean to upset you. Do you want to wait in the lobby while I finish on my own?"

"Are you kidding?" She looked at the ceiling, as if tipping up her eyes would keep the tears inside. "I want to be here. Don't take this away from me," she said softly.

"Okay." I kissed her hair. Well, I kissed the black wig she had on. It felt funny, like the strands were made of thin plastic. I much preferred her soft blonde tresses between my fingers and against my lips, but I wasn't going to get too close to her.

She swallowed and patted at her cheeks and under her eyes before we went into the next room.

The afternoon passed quickly as we laughed and joked with the children. Some were too sick to sit up; some had more energy than they knew what to do with. I wished the hospital had some kind of indoor playground. Even the toddlers would enjoy a swing.

I was thinking through how to make this happen when Ashely said something that caught my attention. "...opening up soon. You should apply."

"What?" I inserted myself into their conversation.

"It's just"—Ashely's eyes darted between the two of us—"we've gotten a grant that will allow us to hire another nutritionist—this one specifically for the children's wing. The money should come through at the end of the month, but they're already taking applications." Ashely stopped at the nurses' station. We were done with our round.

"How come I haven't seen the job posted anywhere?" asked Lottie. She leaned forward intently.

I wasn't sure I liked this. Having Lottie work with the Wolves would mean she and I were on the same schedule. I'd see her in the front office. She'd be close. The off-season could be ours. I mean, if we were really together and stuff.

If she worked here...I scrunched up my face, trying to figure out what that would look like. A long-distance relationship—you know, if we continued with the facade and everything.

"If you're interested, I can give you the ID number for the job and you can look it up on our website."

"Y—"

"Thanks," I butted in, "but we're good." I sounded sharp, and I knew it. Maybe being dressed like this and only saying two-word sentences for hours had gotten to me.

"Jaxson, a job at the hospital would be really good for me." She spoke through her teeth, telling me to butt out.

I should have, but I didn't like the idea of Lottie working here when I had to go back to Texas. "I know, dear, but we need to think about what's good for *us*. It's part of being a couple."

Lottie smiled too big and grabbed my arm. "Let me have a talk with my *thick-headed* helper here. Can I call you later?"

"Sure." Ashley kept her gaze on the floor, obviously uncomfortable with our disagreeing in front of her. "Here's my number." She handed over her business card.

Lottie glanced down at her outfit, realizing she didn't have so much as a pocket to put it in. She thanked Ashely, who hurried off to her next appointment.

"Looks like you don't have a place to put that." I smirked. "Maybe it's a sign."

She glared back at me and tucked it into her long boot. Tugging me down the hall, she found a supply closet and shoved me inside.

As soon as the door shut, we were in total darkness. I knew there was a light switch somewhere, but I was afraid to put my hands out and start groping around, for fear that I'd accidentally grab the wrong thing.

"What is the matter with you?" Lottie hissed not far from me.

My body reacted to her nearness, and my arms reached for her.

"The whole reason we're doing this is so you can get a job. Why do you even need to think about applying at the hospital?"

She let out a frustrated sound. "Because there's no guarantee, Jaxson. Just because you put my name in doesn't mean they'll hire me. More likely than not, they'll fly me out for a cursory interview and then hire someone else." She sighed. "It seems that I always need someone else to help me. This would be the first time that I wasn't the loser of the family."

I coughed at her words. She couldn't possibly think that. "You're not the loser of the family," I said as I shifted closer to her. The need to protect her, even from herself, swelled in my chest. I could hear her insecurities in her tone, and they dropped my defenses. I was powerless when it came to Lottie—and even weaker when she was hurting. "They have to hire you." I tried to speak with as much surety as I could.

"No, they don't," she whispered. I felt her shift against my fingers, and out of instinct, I made contact with her side and tugged her closer.

"Everyone in my family is successful and settled. I'll always be the last in line," she murmured.

"Lottie, that's not true." I leaned down so I could talk low in her ear. I wanted her to hear me. To understand what I was feeling toward her. I knew getting this close to her was a mistake. There were no cameras around. There were no witness. It was just me and her.

There was nothing *fake* about what I was feeling. I inhaled as I felt her warmth wash over me. The smell of sunscreen filled my senses. She must have put it on before going out to the pool that morning. It was everything I was beginning to love about Lottie. She was down-to-earth and yet beautiful in a way she didn't understand. But everyone who even spent five seconds in her presence could feel it. Sense it.

Heck, half the children's wing at this hospital was in love with her, and they'd only spent five minutes with her.

Suddenly, a realization dawned on me. At the end of this charade, I was going to have to walk away. She wasn't mine, not really. There was going to come a point where she was going to move on with her life. Move on with her heart.

And suddenly, leaving this closet didn't seem like something I could do. Once we left, we were going to be that much closer to breaking up. And even though for Lottie it would be fake, for me, I was beginning to fear that it would be too real.

"You're amazing," I whispered as I inched closer to her. My hands found her waist, and to my surprise, she allowed me to keep them there. "The Wolves are going to see that within the first three seconds of meeting you."

"You're only saying that because you're fake-dating me. And I'm pretty sure NFL VIP and loser isn't the kind of headline you want to make," she whispered and then giggled at her own joke.

Which made her even more adorable.

A sense of warmth rushed through me, and I couldn't help but lean in. She thought she was a loser? Was she kidding me?

"You're not a loser," I growled out as my hands found her lower back and I pulled her closer to me. "You're beautiful, kind, generous. Other women don't hold a candle to you." I slipped one hand free from her back and rested it against her cheek. It wasn't like I'd never kissed in the dark before, but this time it felt different. I wanted to get it right. There was no way I was screwing this kiss up.

"Jaxson," she whispered, emotions coating her words.

Suddenly the mood shifted, and I didn't wait to respond. Heat built inside of me, and all I could think about was how warm and soft she was, how her lips would taste. How familiar they were pressed to mine.

"Lottie," I said, my voice dropping a few octaves.

She wasn't pulling back. She wasn't stopping this. She had to feel the electricity as it pulsed through me. I could only assume what I so desperately wanted to think. She wanted this kiss too.

I dipped my head and found her lips. Unlike our other kisses, this one was hot and passionate. My hands found her hips again, and I ran them up and down her back, feeling the curves underneath her costume. She moaned softly, and I deepened the kiss, backing her up against the wall. Moving with urgency, I kissed her neck, trailing kisses along her jaw and then going right back to her talented lips.

The door opened, but it didn't register to me what that meant until I was blinded by the lights. Lottie and I shrank away, putting our hands up over our eyes.

"Seriously?" asked Carter. He stood in the doorway, wearing his snow-white doctor's coat and looking totally ticked off. "Is this part of the scheme? You needed some pictures of you making out in weird places?" He waved his hand around indicating the shelves of medical supplies. "It's bad enough there are new articles about you two every day—you don't have to feed the fire."

"Carter, what are you doing here?" Lottie answered his question with one of her own. I glanced down at her, and my eyes about bugged out of my head. Her face was smeared with my green makeup. The evidence of what we'd done was plain as day.

"Jeff from security called and said he saw you sneaking in here with some guy."

Lottie huffed. "First of all, we weren't sneaking. Second of all, we came in here so I could tell him off for being an idiot." She hooked her thumb at me.

Carter gave her a dubious look. "Really?"

I shook my head at her, warning her off from digging her heels into that stretch of the truth.

She didn't take my warning. "Yeah, so unless you want me to give you what for, too, you'd better shoo." She glared.

Carter snickered. "In that case, the next time you tell a guy off, try not to let him smear his makeup on you." With that, he flipped off the lights and shut the door behind him.

Lottie gasped. She scrambled for the light switch, bumping into me in the process. When the lights came on, she flipped around, her eyes wide. "Is it really that bad?" She raised her palms but didn't touch them to her cheeks as if she was afraid she'd smudge what was there.

I pulled the corners of my mouth down and shook my head. "It's…"

She spied some shiny medical equipment on the shelf behind me and grabbed for it. "Oh. My. Gosh. I look like a sick Smurf."

"I think you look cute."

She smacked me in the stomach and groaned. "The whole world's going to know about this."

"That's kind of the point." I patted her back.

"You don't understand." She dropped her head and carefully pinched the bridge of her nose.

I was at a loss. "Technically, we're dating and in love. So, what's the problem?"

She huffed. "The problem is, you're not the one who will end up on another meme."

"Oh." She had a point.

"Yeah. *Oh.*"

"It won't be that bad." I brushed the long black hair over her shoulder. "I'll bet it says something like 'Jaxson Jagger: so yummy.'"

She shook her head.

I was warming up to the subject and the fact that I might get a smile out of her. "Or maybe it will say, 'I don't always make out in supply closets, but when I do, it's with Jaxson Jagger.'"

"That's awful!" She smacked my stomach again. A light went on in her eyes. "Or they'll put a picture of me side by side with this image and say, 'One week with Jaxson Jagger.'"

I tickled her side, and she squealed, laughing. "She's all that and a bowl of guacamole."

"I dated Jaxson Jagger and all I got was this rash," she gasped through her giggles.

I tickled her more, moving from her side to her collarbone and back faster than she could move her arms to block me. "Okay!" she gasped. "Okay. Uncle."

I let up but didn't back away. "Don't ever think you're not as good as your brothers and sister." I ran my finger down her jaw. "You're..." I could hardly think of the words as a dozen moments from that afternoon flashed through my mind. "You leave me speechless."

She smiled shyly. The door opened, and a female voice yelped, "Sorry!"

Lottie rolled her eyes. "We have to get out of here."

I dug through a few bins and came up with a tub of baby wipes. "Here, try this."

A few minutes later she was ready to go.

It wasn't until later that night, as I was staring up at my ceiling and trying not to think of Lottie a few yards away, that I realized we'd kissed without cameras, or an audience, or even an agenda. Everything that happened in that supply closet was real.

And the thought scared the crap out of me.

13

LOTTIE

*A*s was his pattern, Jaxson disappeared after our *incredible* make-out session in the supply closet. Only, this time, he had to go. The team was called back to Austin, and NFL players go running when the team calls.

I was okay with him leaving because it was for his job and because, instead of taking off without a word, he left me with a sweet smile and a light hug. Which was about all he could do with Liam standing there.

Still, it sent butterflies wild inside of my stomach.

I liked that he and Liam were traveling together and on the same team. They'd keep each other out of trouble. Plus, there was no way Liam would let Jaxson do anything that would smear my name. As far as he was concerned, Jaxson was off-limits to the ladies until we ended our fake relationship. He'd stand guard and shoo off the groupies.

I figured that, after all the grief he'd given us about this publicity stunt and the kiss at the football field, Liam owed me.

Jaxson and I didn't talk about our supply-closet rendezvous, but I could see that mischievous glint in his eyes when he looked at me. He'd felt something, just like I had. And even though the words hadn't been spoken, I knew he cared about me because of the way he'd held me. There's something different about being held by someone I connected with and being held by someone who just wanted to kiss. Jaxson had held me safe.

Guys don't do that for their fake girlfriends.

With the men out of the house, Violet bid us a fond farewell. I didn't mourn her leaving. I helped pack her suitcase and offered to drive her to the airport. She declined, flicked her hair out of her face, and called an Uber. When Liam got back, I was going to have a heart-to-heart with my brother about his taste in women.

We'd reached the intervention point.

Monday was depressingly average. Like the day after returning home from a trip to Disneyland. Falling back into a routine made my muscles sigh with boredom. On Tuesday, Mom hosted a charity for the club she and Dad were members of. Penny was on day shifts now, and I watched Frozen on a loop with Katie. Suzie was at work and couldn't come over to dissect my closet kisses and help me sort through my feelings.

By Thursday, I could have used a good girl talk because I hadn't heard from Jaxson. I couldn't text him first. I didn't want to be a needy fake girlfriend who constantly asked if he thought I was beautiful and if he missed me.

But it sure would have been nice if he'd brought it up.

The one bright spot of my week without him was that I'd finally gotten the green makeup out of my hair. Somehow the color had gotten under the wig at the back of my neck and died my blonde hair. Every time I looked at it, I'd frown and then grin like an idiot thinking about how it got there.

The guys were due to arrive Saturday—time undisclosed.

Seriously, I was going to have to talk with Jaxson about his lack of communication in this fake relationship. I got up and dressed as cute and casual as I could. I wanted to look good without looking like I was trying too hard.

Penny had a great opportunity open up to do in-home care for an elderly patient. It paid great, but she would have to work at both the hospital and the other job for a couple weeks to make the transition. She told me again and again how grateful she was that I came home when I did, that I was saving her bacon. But I could see how hard it was on her to be away from her daughter.

When the doorbell rang on Saturday afternoon, I abandoned my pretzel chips and hummus and padded over to the front door. I straightened my messy bun and ran my tongue over my teeth to make sure they were clear. I pulled open the door...

And choked on my own spit.

Mrs. Jagger stood in front of me with her hands clasped together. She was dressed nice for someone who had just gotten off a plane. The designer scarf tied around her neck matched her blouse and pencil skirt. And her hair was as orderly as a line of soldiers ready for inspection. There was a carry-on bag, in the same shade of navy blue as her skirt, sitting next to her.

She was intimidating and unexpected, and I was as scrambled as eggs.

What was she doing here?

"H-hey, Mrs. Jagger," I said as I stepped onto the front stoop to greet her. I lifted my hand to shake hers but then changed directions and moved in for a hug. I'm sure I looked like some crazed animatronic robot. But I wasn't sure what the protocol was when meeting your fake boyfriend's estranged parent. She was my fake in-law, right? Or no?

Crap.

Where was Jaxson? He should be home by now.

Maybe he'd gotten wind of his mom's arrival and decided to steer clear.

Chicken. I'd wring his neck if he left me to deal with this awkward-at-best situation on my own on purpose.

Thankfully, Mrs. Jagger was gracious and leaned in and hugged me.

That was a good sign.

"My, you have grown up," she said as she ran her gaze over me like an adoring parent.

My cheeks flushed as I nodded and then shook my head.

What was my problem? *Pick a lane, Lottie. She's not going to be impressed with your flip-flopping.*

I smiled and let out my breath slowly. "Thanks. You too. It's been a long time." I blinked a few times as my response replayed in my head. Did I just tell Mrs. Jagger that she looked grown up? But, before I could retrace my steps, I caught her sad expression as she looked at the front door of my house. Something in her look, regret maybe, had me holding my tongue.

"It has," she said in a low tone.

I searched my brain for something intelligent to say, something that would put her sorrows in her suitcase and leave them there. "How's Germany?"

She considered me for a moment. "It was beautiful, especially at Christmas, but we moved back to the States three years ago."

"You did?" I bit my cheek. Shouldn't a girlfriend know where her boyfriend's family lived? For that matter, did Jaxson know?

Jaxson didn't really talk a lot about his family. But I knew it bothered him that his family wasn't around, and he'd been pretty upset when they moved away without him. He didn't show it in front of people back then. If anyone asked, he told them he won the jackpot being able to live with us. I guess he had, considering the way his career turned out. My parents had a lot to do with that.

But there was a night, maybe the first night he moved in, that I caught him in the garage, beating the crap out of our punching bag and swearing at his father who wasn't present. It was almost like he wanted to beat up his dad. And my heart ached for him as he choked back sorrow and his back heaved with the effort. I never told him that I'd seen him that night. I didn't think it was something he wanted known.

Besides, I hadn't understood what was so bad about his dad until later.

The Jaggers bled Marines blue, and the fact that Jaxson didn't go into the military really bothered his family. Not just his dad but his brothers and sister too. It had to be hard growing up with that kind of conditional love. Sure, I was the disappointment of my family, but at least they loved me no matter what. And they didn't pack up and leave me in the dust when I didn't do what they said.

"I sent your mother a change of address. We're in California..." She trailed off into a state of reverie, so I remained quiet. There was no sense sticking my foot back in my mouth or getting in the middle of her and Jaxson's communications—or lack of them.

After a moment. Mrs. Jagger seemed to come back to earth as she turned her attention over to me and smiled again. She had a determined set to her jaw as she wrapped her fingers around the handle of her suitcase and stepped toward the door.

"Is my son h-home?" she asked, stuttering on the last word.

Realizing that I was being a horrible hostess, I hurried to push the front door open and ushered her into the front entryway.

Katie must have been curious about who was here because I found her raised up on her tiptoes, peeking through the side window. As soon as I neared, she scampered to stand behind my legs and peek out at Mrs. Jagger, who rolled her suitcase into the foyer.

"Jaxson's actually gone at the moment. They had this big new exposé and the whole team went to Austin. I'm expecting them home today."

Just as the words left my lips, my stomach twisted. Was I bothered by the fact that Jaxson hadn't texted, emailed, or sent a carrier pigeon? Yes, yes I was. Because you're supposed to text your fake girlfriend, darn it. I didn't get so much as an emoji or GIF or an honorable mention on his social media account.

And I would know. I stalked every single platform. I was privy to his workouts and dinners with the team, but there wasn't any mention of me.

Nada.

My one consolation was that there weren't any other women either.

And Liam's account didn't have a thing about Violet.

Oh my gosh, I was becoming Violet. I needed to get a grip.

Mrs. Jagger sighed as she glanced around. Her eyes dropped to

Katie and then moved around and then came back to her. It was almost like she couldn't help but want to stare at the little girl. Which wasn't doing much for Katie's comfort. Her arms tightened around my leg.

"That is disappointing," Mrs. Jagger whispered.

Confused at what she was doing here, I stuck my hand out in the direction of the kitchen. "Would you like a drink?" I asked. She'd brought a suitcase, but I was sure she wasn't planning on staying here —Mom would have said something. Then again, Jaxson had shown up without warning and moved right in, so what did I know? Maybe it was a family trait. I hoped not. I had a hard enough time being normal around this woman on the front porch for a short hello; living with her could bring out my clumsy side. Since my ankle had only recently healed from the last time I'd stumbled, I wasn't looking forward to a repeat.

"Joice box," Katie said as she peeked out from behind my legs. "We hawve joice box."

A smile unlike any I'd ever seen on Mrs. Jagger before spread over her lips. It was as if she'd found her reason for being alive in the big blue eyes of my niece. She crouched down, dropping one knee slightly and turning to the side in an elegant move. I was amazed at her poise since she wore three-inch heels and a pencil skirt. I would have fallen over if I'd tried on the shoes, let alone changed my center of gravity. She perched there as she peered around at Katie, who had shrunk behind my legs.

"Do you have fruit punch? That's my favorite," she whispered. I could see a craving in her eyes for this little girl to speak to her. She held Katie's gaze.

To my surprise, Katie rounded my legs and reached for Mrs. Jagger's hand.

"Fwollow me," Katie said in a serious voice as she took them both toward the kitchen.

Once we were settled at the bar, Katie busied herself getting drinks and fruit snacks for everyone. She pulled her tea set out of the bottom shelf in the pantry and arranged plates and cups in front of us while

Mrs. Jagger looked on with adoration. I hadn't realized she was such a softie, and it kind of made me like her more.

I cut open the juice boxes and poured them into Katie's tea kettle, and we all settled down together like proper ladies. Mrs. Jagger kept her ankles crossed and sipped daintily, her pinky extended just as Katie instructed.

I slurped every now and again to give Katie the opportunity to instruct me on proper tea party etiquette. Katie kept Mrs. Jagger's attention as she talked about dolls, barbies, and, of course, *Frozen*. Mrs. Jagger offered her opinion on Barbie's dress—it was a classic that would stand the test of time. And admitted she hadn't seen *Frozen* yet, which earned her another ten minutes of "Tristoph" conversation. Katie's crush may have moved into obsession territory.

While Katie jabbered on, my mind spun with questions.

Not all of them were polite questions. Like, "What are you doing here?" and "Are you and Jaxson on speaking terms?" I couldn't ask those, though I might be able to skirt the issue and maybe she'd volunteer the information.

It was nice, sitting back and allowing someone else be Katie's play buddy for a few minutes. I loved my niece more than I loved hot fudge on ice cream, but I'd had enough tea parties this last summer to last me a lifetime.

After about an hour, Katie grew tired and made her way back into the living room, leaving me and Mrs. Jagger alone. I brewed a pot of coffee and took two mugs to the table. I sipped from my mug as I waited for her to start. After all, she was the one who had shown up on my doorstep, and I was at a loss as to what to say.

"I went off coffee when I was expecting." She looked pointedly at my cup.

I cocked my head to the side. What a weird thing to say. "That's probably a good idea." It came out more as a question than a statement.

"I saw the article about you and Jaxson," she said as she dragged her finger along the rim of the mug.

I swallowed and nodded. Telling my family that we were in a fake relationship was one thing, but I had no frame of reference for trusting Mrs. Jagger with that information. Gossip sites paid heavily for insider news, and she could be here as a spy.

But she was Jaxson's *mother*. Guilt made a nice little home inside of me as I contemplated the implications of her believing I was actually her son's devoted and loving girlfriend. The way she was looking at me, shy, uncertain of her welcome, hopeful even. It was like she wanted me to be in her family, wanted us to be friends.

Why the heck didn't Jaxson warn her when this whole thing started?

"What article?" I prodded, waiting to see what she said. There was a slim chance that she'd look me right in the eye and call my bluff. I was cool with that. If she guessed this was fake, then I'd be off the hook. Right?

I could handle her saying that her son would never be interested in a girl like me way easier than her hoping that Jaxson and I were an item. Because if she wanted us together, then she was in for a world of disappointment.

So whatever was on her mind was strong enough to get her on an airplane to fly out here from California and say the words to my face.

A lump formed in my throat, stopping me from making any sound. It wasn't tears, and it wasn't anger—it was fear.

Two types of fear to be exact.

Fear of being rejected by Jaxson's mom. I liked him—a lot. Was even falling in love with him. What would happen to us if she disapproved? I mean, part of me hoped that we could take the "fake" out of our relationship at some point, maybe just forget it was there and never go through the breakup.

I know, I live in a dream world.

The other fear was of being accepted by Mrs. Jagger. Because then I was a liar, and my shot of being a part of that family was next to zero.

I was in a no-win situation and ready to pass out from lack of breath.

She grew quiet as she took in a slow breath. "I'm so happy he's found a good girl." Her gaze was downturned and her voice broke with all the hopes and dreams of a mother's heart.

Acceptance it was. Which meant I was the bad guy.

Curses.

I blinked a few times as I took in her words and the tentative way she met my gaze. I wanted to tell her that it was all for show. That I was, in fact, not the good girl she'd been hoping and maybe even praying for, for her long-lost son; the words clung to my throat. I just couldn't stomp on that spark of joy in her eyes. Because that joy wasn't just because of me—it was for Jaxson. Her love for him shone through her smile like the sun breaking through the clouds on a winter day.

"And the fact that you're engaged? I had to fly here and congratulate you myself."

A ringing started in my ears as I stared at Mrs. Jagger. I knew she was speaking, I just couldn't process her words. "I'm...we're...what?" I stammered out. Engaged? Shoot—she thought we were getting married. The welcome to the family hugs and smiles suddenly made all the sense in the world. I needed to stop this now. I opened my mouth, but she spoke before I could get a word out.

"I know I haven't been the best mother, and I'm not going to lie, his father is still bitter. But I'm tired of not having my son in my life."

Well shucks. What could I say to that?

"And with your engagement, the new baby, and Katie?" She reached over and rested her hand on mine. "I swear I will be the best grandmother."

Whoa. Whoa, whoa, whoa.

What was happening right now?

"Do you think you can talk to Jax for me? I hope we can start over. I'm just worried that he hates me for not coming sooner."

"Katie's my niece." I ventured. That much had been released to the press, and I knew it was safe to get that in the open. She'd read about it eventually anyway. Although, it sounded like she was a one-site gal. Depending on which one she followed, there could be problems.

"Oh." She turned and looked in the direction Katie had gone only moments before. It felt like years. "She's so sweet." She chuckled. "I kept looking for some of Jaxson in her, but I didn't see it. I guess you can't believe everything you read. Well, there's always the little one on the way. Tell me how you're feeling. Oh, I almost forgot."

She ran back to the entryway, where she'd left her suitcase, and came back with a hand-crocheted blanket. It was cream with a raspberry edge and so beautiful. The hours it must have taken for her to craft something so precious were like arrows of guilt.

"I made this." She held it close. "I know you don't know if you're having a boy or a girl, but I have so much love for this little one in my heart." She handed me the blanket. "If it's a boy, I'll make another. But, please accept it."

My mouth was dry, and no amount of swallowing helped. I raked through my brain, but I couldn't find the words. Pregnant? I was going to kill all reporters.

And then I was going to kill Jaxson.

It didn't help that Mrs. Jagger looked so happy. There were actual tears in her eyes.

And call me crazy, but I didn't want to go down as the person who took away her first grandchild.

"Okay," I managed to get out. Everything around me felt as if it were spinning. I felt like I was on a boat in the water, swirling into a whirlpool of death. I knew I should say something. Contradict what she thought and tear her dreams in two, but I couldn't find the words.

"Nantie?" Katie called from the living room.

I stood so fast that the chair shot out from behind me and clattered to the floor. I set the blanket on the table and sheepishly picked up the chair and bowed to Mrs. Jagger like a lowly chambermaid standing before a queen. I had to get out of there—now. "Excuse me," I mumbled, sprinting to the living room, where I found Katie bouncing on the couch.

"I wanna bath," she said.

I didn't have the energy to tell her to get off the couch for the hundredth time that week. She'd decided it was her favorite jumping spot, and Penny wanted that out of her head ASAP.

Instead of reprimanding her, I grabbed her, hoisted her over my shoulder, and headed up the stairs. "I'll be back in a little bit," I called to Mrs. Jagger, who was still sitting at the table with her head tipped down and her shoulders rounded. She fingered the blanket, brushing her hand over it as one would the soft fuzz on a baby's head.

My entire heart ached at her posture. The poor woman. I knew a lot of Jaxson's issues stemmed from his father. Mrs. Jagger was just trying to keep the peace by following Colonel Jagger's orders. How much had she given up over the years because of her husband's gruffness and the orders he issued? Had anyone protected her heart? Loved her? Shown her a bit of tenderness? Babies didn't give love, but they snuggled and smiled and cooed and pretty much made the world a brighter place.

How could I be the person who took the sunshine from her?

I slipped into Penny's room with Katie. She had a suite with a queen bed in her room and an adjacent smaller room for Katie. It used to be a walk-in closet with a sitting area but was large enough for Katie's princess bed and a dresser.

They had a private bathroom that smelled like strawberry shampoo. I turned on the water to fill the large whirlpool tub. Katie squealed with delight and said, "Bubbwles!"

"You got it, kid!" She'd gotten me out of an awkward situation. I would have fed her cookies in the tub if she'd asked for them.

Normally we saved baths for nighttime, but right now, I needed a chance to do some research and a moment to gather my thoughts. This pit was deep, and it got deeper with every moment.

I spent Katie's entire bath chewing on my fingernails and doing some investigation on my phone. The old article about Katie being our love child was still up. That same site had a picture of us in costume going into the women's center at the hospital last week. I groaned. Of course there was no mention of the construction that forced us through those doors. We looked like idiots trying to evade the paparazzi by dressing like superheroes. I guess I knew which site Mrs. Jagger followed.

I put my phone away before the memes started to show up.

By the time I finished reading the speculative articles, I was angry.

Angry at the tabloids who were trying to make a buck off the juiciest story.

Angry at the person who had sent in the photo.

Angry at Jaxson for not warning his family and for not texting me all week and for a half dozen other things that I hadn't put complete thoughts to yet. It was kind of amazing how angry I could be with him while looking forward to seeing his face again.

And I was angry at myself for thinking any of these lies were a good idea in the first place. No job was worth this.

I'd known there was a possibility that people would get hurt, I just didn't figure that it would be Jaxson's mom who would be crushed. Jaxson and I weren't engaged, and there was no baby at the end of this. No little bundle of joy to soften the blow.

She was going to return to California empty-handed.

Oh my gosh, the blanket. What was she going to do with the blanket? Surely, she wouldn't want me to keep it. Every time she looked at it, she'd be reminded of what a horrible thing I'd done.

Once Katie was out of the tub and in her Elsa nightgown, we made our way back down to the living room. I'd resigned myself to being the one to tell Mrs. Jagger the truth. I mean, I couldn't sit here and plan a baby shower or anything, knowing that there wasn't a baby. Maybe I could just tell her the papers had exaggerated and let her know what we were really doing at the hospital. Then I'd let Jaxson tell her the rest. If I talked slowly enough, he might be home by the time I finished.

I wandered through the front room, thinking she might have settled in there, but she was nowhere to be found. There was a note in the kitchen—on the blanket.

She was going to visit some old friends, but she would be back later tonight. She also apologized that she hadn't asked before, but she wondered if she could stay at our house. I ran to the entryway, and sure enough, her suitcase waited by the closet.

Goodie.

I went back to the kitchen and re-read her note, tapping my

fingers nervously on the counter. I didn't like the fact that hours were going to pass before I could clear up our misunderstanding—er, part of our misunderstanding.

With the ulcer that was forming in my stomach, I knew there was a good chance that I was going to be an emotional basket case by the time she returned.

I blew out my breath as I collapsed on the couch next to Katie, burying my face in one of the throw pillows. I swallowed as I pulled my feet up underneath me and laid my head back.

The thought of Jaxson and I being engaged, like his mother thought, made me feel light-headed. Katie burrowed under my arm and snuggled close. My heart pounded as I thought about having a child of my own.

That his mother could actually picture Jaxson and me being married and, at some point, having children was a huge compliment.

And the feeling of completeness that sparked inside of me made me groan. I knew it was a lie—all of it. I knew that Jaxson wasn't mine and I wasn't his. I'd been pretending. Having fun, as Suzie said. I'd let down my guard and opened my heart. I'd played the game.

Every part of my being—every part of my soul, wanted to believe that what Jaxson's mom thought was actually true.

And that terrified me.

I wasn't ready to fall in love with Jaxson Jagger, but deep down I knew it didn't matter.

I already had.

Which meant that something had to change. I wasn't quite sure what, but I knew that I couldn't continue on the way we were.

14

JAXSON

"Meet me in a half hour at Del Sol?" I sent the text off to Lottie as soon as we landed and then tucked my phone in my back pocket before Liam could see.

He'd been glued to my side all week, like a slice of bread covered in peanut butter. I didn't know if Carter had told him about the kissing session at the hospital, and I certainly wasn't going to bring it up. So I put up with his watchdog behavior even though it meant I didn't have a second of my own to call or text Lottie.

I was going through withdrawal.

My phone lit up with messages as we got off the plane. I'd wait until I was alone to look through them.

Thankfully, I had a car in long-term parking, which meant this ridiculous charade between Liam and me could stop. If he thought he was going to drive me home and sit next to me on the couch, he had another thing coming.

"I'll see you at home?" he asked as we boarded the shuttle to the parking garage.

I shook my head. "I think I'll grab a bite to eat. Want me to bring you something?" I was trying to make it clear he wasn't invited without actually having to say the words.

He hung onto the bar as the shuttle started off. "I'm good. Mom usually has something in the fridge."

"Kay. I need some more of that protein powder too." I stared out the window, hoping the excitement charging inside of me like an offensive line pushing toward the end zone didn't come across. The energy was bouncing all over my skin and making it difficult to stand still.

He gave me a pointed look. "You're not sneaking off to meet up with a woman, are you?"

"W-what?" I grabbed onto the bar in front of me as we took a crazy turn. The elderly woman driving swiped at her glasses and blinked several times. How long had she been on shift? Thankfully, my car was out of harm's way in the middle of a row.

"Look, I know you are true to your word, but hanging with my little sister isn't exactly the life you're used to. And I get that your situation is…" He looked around, and I did too. A preteen boy was staring at the two of us, but he was the only one paying any attention. "… unique. But that doesn't mean you can cheat on her."

I scoffed before I even thought about my response. "Bro, I would never."

"Even though you guys aren't…" he pushed.

I shook my head. "I can honestly say that since she and I started *dating*," this talking in code was getting on my nerves. "I haven't thought of another woman. It's not even a temptation." The answer was spot on, truer than true, and right from my heart.

His chin jerked back.

My blood simmered. "Why do you think I'd do that?" I thought he knew me. I thought he respected me.

"I don't know. You just always have these hot little ladies hanging on you."

"Is that why you've been my shadow this week?"

He ducked his head. "Lottie's taking a lot of bad press about this thing between you two. It would devastate her to be publicly scorned by a cheating boyfriend."

"I would never do that to her. Publicly or otherwise." The sincerity in my tone was too strong. It spoke of feelings I had yet to identify or accept. And I certainly wasn't ready to throw them out there for Liam to refute. He was good at denial. Case in point: he refused to see that Violet was using him for his fame. She was in love all right, in love with seeing herself on social media and news outlets.

We came to stop D, and I grabbed my carry-on. "This is my stop. I'll see you later."

Liam said goodbye with a chin lift, and I was finally free. I took out my phone, intent on meeting up with Lottie ASAP. But her name wasn't at the top of the call list.

It was my mom.

I swore under my breath.

My mom rarely called. And when she did, it was to let me know that one of my siblings was being sent off to some far away country to protect our freedom. She'd ask me to pray for them while they were gone. I'd agree because I loved my brothers and sister. Growing up in a big family and moving as much as we did, made them my best friends. Until I'd decided to break the family mold. Now we hardly talked. Although, I wondered if that was as much Dad's fault as it was anybody's. He was the type of man who would have told them to leave me alone, to let me wallow in my loneliness, "solitary confinement changed behavior."

I was sick just thinking about the ways he could have poisoned them against me.

And what about my mother? Where was she in all this?

I was still mad she'd left me behind all those years ago. Like my emotions were stuck in the form of a seventeen-year-old boy with long hair and a bad attitude.

Bless her, she tried. She'd asked about football and who I was dating. I'd play the big man on campus routine and joke about all the women who couldn't get enough of me—acting like I was wanted by thousands, and she was dumb for not wanting me back then.

I stopped at my car and glared at the reflection in the window.

Look what you're missing out on, Mom. Just seeing her name on my screen sent me to a bad place.

What I needed was some sunshine.

I needed Lottie.

Her text was short and to the point: "Sure." Casual. Unconcerned with games or issues. That's what I liked about her. She was laid-back and fun. I was already swimming to the top of the funk Mom had spiraled me into.

Lottie was waiting for me at the restaurant. I found her at a table, shredding a napkin. "Hey there, beautiful." I touched her arm and guided her out of the chair and into my arms. I pulled her in, soaking up the acceptance and the caring and her general sense of joy. Which, I realized as I tuned in to her, was muffled by stress.

"I have great news," I said, hoping to lift the worry off of her. I pulled out her chair so she could sit down and took the spot right next to her so I could hold her hand. She stared at our entwined fingers. "I talked to the front office about you and forwarded them that e-resume you have online. They were really excited about you and said they'd call in the next week or so to set up an interview." I grinned, feeling like her knight in shining football pads. "I thought, maybe, we could fly down and I could show you around."

Two lines appeared between her eyes. "Fly down? Like, together?" There was a hesitancy to her voice that caused the hairs on the back of my neck to stand up. Almost like she still believed that all of this was fake. "You just got back."

I'd been in that closet with her. I knew how she felt about me. None of this was fake anymore.

"Yeah, but I don't mind." I ran my thumb over her soft knuckles. Her skin was like rose petals. I internally laughed at myself. I'd felt rose petals like once in my life and here I was thinking of them and her together. I was acting like a love-sick puppy.

But I didn't care.

"What about your mom?" she asked, her voice high and tight. "And the new rumors going around?"

Instantly, the air around us tightened. I felt confused and worried —no longer relaxed and at ease. I let go of her hand and ran my suddenly moist palms down my pant legs. "What about Mom? What rumors?"

"She just got here. I didn't think—"

"Wait!" I held up a palm, cutting her off. "What are you talking about?"

She turned in her seat and opened her purse, which was hanging over the back of the chair. From inside, she pulled out a baby blanket done in cream and pink. She set it on the table where our hands had been. With a thick swallow she explained, "There's a new article floating around, claiming that I'm pregnant with your baby." Her phone landed next to the blanket. The image onscreen was the two of us in costume going into the women's center of the hospital. The headline read, "Surprise Baby!"

I shook my head. "No one believes this stuff. But I'll have Brent put out a statement. It will go away in 24 hours."

She laid her palm on the blanket. "Your mom made this for her grandchild."

I stared at her hand on top of the blanket. "You're kidding?"

"Jaxson, she cried with joy." Lottie's eyes misted over. "I didn't know what to tell her. I couldn't…" She leaned forward. "I couldn't break her heart and tell her this was all a lie," she whispered. "You need to explain things to her."

I leaned back in my chair. The blanket freaked me out on so many levels.

One. The idea of Lottie carrying my child had not caused panic or even a general sense of unease. I'd been—if I had to pick an emotion—excited. That reaction alone was enough to send me reeling.

Two. My mom wasn't a nurturer. She wasn't allowed to be. We kids were to buck up and quit crying. I'd never heard or seen my mother cry for joy or sadness. If she could make tears, then she'd kept them hidden from us.

Another part of what Lottie'd said sunk in. "I don't have to explain anything to her."

She shook her head. "Jaxson, you have to tell her the truth."

My protect-myself instincts roared to life like an engine when the key turns. "She doesn't need to know the truth."

Lottie blinked. "It's okay. She's family."

I shook my head. "No. The McKnights are my family. She's just the woman who gave birth to me."

Lottie gasped. "Jaxson!"

"It's true. She didn't want me back then, and she doesn't want me now. All she wants is a grandkid." I shoved the blanket onto Lottie's lap. "And she's not getting that either."

Lottie chewed her lip.

My anger deflated. "It's not you I'm upset at. I'm sorry I got so heated." I reached for her hand once more. "Can we just put this aside for a while?"

Her forehead wrinkled. "You want to *pretend*?"

I lifted a shoulder. I needed space from all this. "This isn't the evening I had in mind."

"Me neither." Her hand slipped out from under mine. She gathered the blanket in her lap and twisted to stuff it back into her bag. "I can't pretend, Jaxson. Not anymore."

A shot of panic sliced through me. "What do you mean?"

"I mean, we said this was fake but there are real people involved, real feelings. I was the only one who was supposed to get hurt. I didn't think—"

"Why would you get hurt?" I globbed onto that question because it seemed the most important. "Lottie, I won't hurt you."

Her eyes clouded with tears. "I don't think you can help it. It's like when you kissed me on graduation and just walked away. You didn't mean to break my heart, but you did. And now, you're even better." She sniffed. "I can't be with you and not fall in love, Jaxson. And now your mom…"

I blinked in shock. Lottie loved me? Then… "What about your job recommendation? What about our deal?"

She stood quickly and tugged her purse strap over her shoulder. "Tell them I found a position in town." A single tear trailed down her cheek. "You can stay at the house. I'll be at Suzie's. Your mom is at our house anyway and she wants to see you." She took a staggering breath. "You should talk to her." With that bit of advice, she wove through the tables and disappeared out the door.

My backside was glued to the chair because my brain didn't have the ability to process everything she'd just said plus tell my legs to get up and run after her.

My phone rang and I answered it without looking at the number. "Lottie, come back. I didn't know—"

A man cleared his throat.

I shut up. This wasn't Lottie. I pulled my phone back and saw the mayor's name on my screen. Wow. My face heated with embarrassment. "Hello?" I asked. I should have made up an excuse, hung up, and bolted after Lottie, but I wasn't sure what to say to her. She wanted me to tell my mom all about our fake relationship, but that would mean admitting I'd done something incredibly stupid. And I couldn't do that in front of my mom. If word got back to my dad, I'd never hear the end of it.

"Jaxson Jagger." The mayor sounded like he was in a good mood. "Listen, I wanted to thank you for being willing to emcee our hospital fundraiser. That stunt you and Lottie pulled the other day, costumes at the women's center, has brought in a lot of PR for us."

I rubbed my forehead. If I could redo anything in this world...

"Anyway, I hate to do this, but I was wondering if you'd be willing to step down."

"Excuse me?"

"It's such a silly thing, but my friend's nephew is coming into town, and he's, well, he's got a lot of friends with a lot of money—Hollywood kind of money. He's willing to emcee, and I think it would be better for the hospital if he were to take the mic."

My heart sank. Dumped twice in one night. "Whatever is best for the hospital, Mayor."

"Wonderful!" The relief in his voice dripped through the line.

We said goodbye and hung up. I laid the phone on the table and stared at it, afraid to check the rest of the messages. My chest was hollow, like my heart had walked out with Lottie.

I glanced up and swallowed my emotions—like a good Jagger would.

I couldn't tell anyone how upset this made me. I couldn't let the heartbreak show because everyone thought it was fake. I had to be a wall. I could do that. I had a lot of practice. I stood up and stumbled into the table, the weight of my loss too heavy. With effort, I stood tall.

I wouldn't get over this. I'd never be over Lottie. She'd shown me what it was like to be loved for being me. She'd filled my days with emotional peace and thrills, too.

"Can I get you something to go?" asked a waitress.

I shook my head. "I'll be fine," I lied, adding a suave smile to my lips that made her giggle. See, I could make this happen. Lottie thought I'd been pretending before, but I'd never been more real than when I was with her.

The pretending would start now—when I had to act like my soul wasn't crumbling.

For once, I was glad I was a Jagger.

1 5

LOTTIE

"I'm such an idiot," I said through my sniffles. I'd curled up on Suzie's couch with a half-eaten carton of fudge, chocolate, cookie dough, marshmallow, brownie batter, could-my-heart-be-any-more-broken ice cream in my lap, a wadded-up tissue in my hand, and a soft-as-a-teddy-bear blanket wrapped around me. I moved to wipe my nose, but when the tissue didn't do its job, I threw it into the nearly full garbage and grabbed another one.

Suzie was such a good friend. She'd taken one look at me and pulled out the expensive tissues. They smelled like soothing lavender and had lotion so my nose wouldn't be raw like the rest of me.

Suzie sat across from me in an armchair, staring. Her face was contorted in a look of pity as she swept her gaze over my messy hair and rumpled pajamas. I sniffled, picked up my spoon, and scooped another bite of chocolate-filled coping skills.

"I mean, what should I do?" I asked as I glanced over at her. "Should I call him? I should call him, right?"

"And say what? That you were kidding and you want to go back to fake-dating him?"

I swallowed a big lump of coldness and gagged out the word "No." Going back to the way things were wasn't an option.

She paused and then sighed as she shifted in her seat. I loved my friend, I did, but she was a no-nonsense kind of person. If something bugged her—a tag on a shirt, a measuring cup without lines, a guy's attitude—she ditched it without regrets. So the fact that I obsessed about Jaxson was annoying. Especially when she'd specifically told me to just have fun.

One look at my puffy eyes and snotty nose said I hadn't listened to her advice. Which probably also annoyed her.

She'd taken me in last night, the blubbering mess that I was; but asking her for new advice when I hadn't used her last bit probably wasn't the smartest move. She was the only person I had right now. My family thought the whole thing was fake. Jaxson's mom thought it was all real. And my mom had tried to warn me off of this scheme, noting my tender heart and previous crush on Jaxson as reasons I would end up in a puddle of gooey tissues when it was all over.

Staying at my house, where my family could see my meltdown, wasn't an option.

Not if I wanted Jaxson to live.

Even though I wanted to hate him right now, I didn't want Liam to kill him.

It was a complicated mess I'd gotten myself into.

I scooped another bite and shoved it into my mouth as tears stung the back of my eyes. I blinked a few times, and they slipped down my cheeks. My throat tightened from the emotions that swam through me.

"Let me get this straight. You broke up with him because his mom thinks you're pregnant and he didn't want to tell her differently?" Suzie tightened her ponytail. I wondered if she thought my general disheveled state would spread like a virus.

I nodded. "That's part of it. I didn't think we'd hurt anyone. It all seemed so innocent. The other part"—I drew in a fortifying breath, this was so hard to admit to myself, let alone another person—"is that he wanted to keep pretending even though things had gotten real—at least for me. And I can't really love a man who fakes loving me back. It's awful."

"Oh, honey," Suzie sighed as she stood and waved for me to get up. "Take a shower. Get dressed. We're going shopping."

I blinked a few times. My mind was cloudy from the overdose of sugar, cocoa, and emotions that swirled around inside me. It took a moment to process what she'd said. Shopping?

"I don't want to go anywhere." I set the ice cream bucket down on the coffee table and pulled one of her throw pillows to my chest.

Suzie stood in front of me with her hands on her hips, staring me down. I squirmed but didn't get up.

"You can't stay here all day."

"Why not?"

"Because, I have to get a gown for the hospital fundraiser." She grabbed my arm and yanked. "And as your best friend, I can't leave you alone at a time like this. So you have to get up and get moving. Besides, you need a dress too."

I moved slightly and groaned. "I'm not going to that," I said.

Suzie narrowed her eyes. "Yes, you are. If you don't, you'll be banished from the McKnight family forever."

I tried to cover my face with my arm. It wasn't that bad. My parents would understand if I couldn't make it to an event. I'd have to have a good reason, though, and a broken heart wasn't one. Besides, as I'd already established, I couldn't tell anyone in my family that my heart was currently in ashes.

Suzie was having none of my refusal. She tugged harder to get me to stand. Realizing that my friend wasn't going to relent, I slowly moved to my feet.

"Jaxson will be there." My voice was barely a whisper.

Suzie shrugged as she situated herself behind me and began to push me toward the bathroom. I was grateful for my friend's monumental efforts on my behalf even though she was being a pain. I needed someone to kick me into action. If not, I was pretty sure my life would consist of eating ice cream and binge-watching Korean dramas until the end of time.

I let her guide me to her bathroom as she spoke. "So he'll be there. You've made your decision and you have to face it." She pulled open the shower curtain and started the water. My scalp yearned for a good shampoo. I'd lather, rinse, and repeat today.

I leaned against the counter and folded my arms. I stared down at the tile as I let her words sink in around me. "I'm not ready."

"Lottie, listen to me. You have two options: Move on, or wallow. I'm all for wallowing. I mean, if you want to move in here, become a hermit, and live off of delivery, I'm game as long as you pay rent and keep your tissues off the floor."

I smirked at her, the image she painted wasn't pretty.

"But"—she held up a finger—"if your family gets wind of your overwhelming sadness because of this breakup, they'll look at Jaxson differently. Do you think he'll feel comfortable being in that house?" Suzie bent down to meet my gaze. "Your family is all Jaxson has. Liam is his best friend. I have a feeling that hurting his little sister is something Liam wouldn't forgive. You'll be the wedge that comes between them."

I nodded numbly.

She sighed as steam began to fill the bathroom. "Without your family's support, Jaxson will be alone in the world. Is that what you want?"

My heart pounded at the thought of Liam's reaction. Of my family treating Jaxson differently. They weren't awful people. They'd still love him, they'd still cheer him on, but there would be a distance there, a distance I'd created.

And Liam? He'd say horrible, mean things, thinking he was standing up for my honor. Maybe their friendship would recover. Maybe. But Jaxson would know he'd crossed a line, and he could pull away from us. Jaxson had a rough relationship with his own family; he didn't need one with mine too. Especially when it wasn't his fault that I'd gone and fallen in love with him. The last thing he wanted was to hurt my family or me—even though that is exactly what he'd done.

Besides, Jaxson was a good guy. He didn't mean for this to happen, didn't know how much I was already invested in an "us" when we'd started. If it came down to it, he wouldn't stick around if he knew I was uncomfortable.

And I didn't want that.

I straightened and sucked in my breath as I focused on Suzie. Her eyebrows raised as she studied me.

I nodded and then stepped out of the way so she'd know she could go. I was going to make this work. Suzie nodded back and left the bathroom. I shut the door behind her and sighed.

The hot water soothed my muscles. Suzie's lotus flower shampoo and conditioner made me feel like a girl again. After a long shower, I dried off. I wrapped a towel around my hair and one around my body. I pulled open the door and a rush of cold air hit me.

Suzie was waiting in her room for me. She'd laid out some clothes for me to wear, a pair of skinny jeans and a loose top. "You can borrow those."

"I would have put on sweats."

"I know."

"Do you want to make all my decisions for a while?"

She laughed.

"No seriously, I feel like I stink at adulting."

"You'll be fine." She grinned. "But I wouldn't mind a say in what you wear to the fundraiser."

"Fine by me." I didn't want to be out of grunge clothes anyway. Then again, maybe getting dressed up would help. The shower had worked like a reset button, stopping the stream of tears that I hadn't been able to stem overnight.

Once I was dressed, I made my way out to the hallway. My phone rang and my heart leapt to my throat with the hope that it was Jaxson. A hundred scenarios played out in my head in the few seconds it took to get my phone out of my pocket—all of them ending with us kissing.

I glanced down at the screen. All the emotions that had been stirred by the idea that it might be Jaxson quickly left my body when I saw my sister's name: *Penny.*

I took a deep breath to calm my body and hit talk. "Hey."

"Lottie? Where are you?" Her voice had an urgency to it I rarely heard.

I padded into Suzie's kitchen and grabbed a water bottle from her fridge. Hydration was important and I'd lost enough liquids over the last 24 hours to leave me wrinkled and aged. "Right now? Suzie's kitchen," I answered.

Penny fake laughed. "What's going on? Why aren't you here? And why is Jaxson walking around like his team just lost the Super Bowl?"

My ears perked at his name. I desperately wanted to ask her for more details. How did she know he was down? Had he talked to his mom yet? Were they both still there? Was his mom being weird or nice to him? Did he ask about me?

I stuffed all the questions into a small mental box and sat on the lid. My sister was one of my most favorite people, but she could read me well. If I was going to sell this whole fake-breakup thing, I'd have to start right now.

"He's probably just getting ready for the cameras. We've decided to call the fake relationship off. He's acting it up for his mom, I'm sure." Ugh! I hated how convincing I sounded, because it meant I believed it. Although, part of me wondered if he'd explained that I wasn't pregnant yet. That was the kick in the pants Mrs. Jagger didn't need.

Penny was silent for a moment. "Uh-huh," she said, dragging out each syllable.

Not wanting my tears to return and not wanting to drag my family into my mess, I decided now was the perfect time to change the subject. "What do you need, Pen?"

She cleared her throat. "I got a call from Evie. She needs some help this afternoon. I hate to tell her no because the job is so new and I'm barely giving her any time as it is since I'm still working at the hospital. As soon as I start full-time with her, I can bring Katie along, but I'm learning the ropes and I can't have the little munchkin running amuck or hanging all over me. Can you please, please take her for a few hours? Mom has to finish up stuff for the fundraiser and can take her later, I just need somewhere for her to go right now."

I tipped my lips away from the phone. "Suze, interested in having a squirt tag along with us at the mall?"

Suzie gave me a *do you even have to ask* look.

I chuckled as I tipped my lips back to the microphone. "Sure. We'll come grab her."

Penny sighed in relief. "Thank you so, so much! I promise, when you have kids, I'll be the best aunt ever."

Normally, I would have chuckled at her comment—or said something to tease her back—but the whole false pregnancy story was still too fresh. I couldn't even muster a half-crazed cackle.

"Lot?" she asked.

I paused. "Yeah?"

There was silence for a moment. The kind that said she was picking her words carefully. I didn't like that at all and braced for what came next.

"Talk to Jaxson. It may have been fake for you, but I don't think it was the same for him. I…I recognize his reaction. It's…" Her voice trailed off, and I waited for her to continue, but she never did.

I wondered if it had something do with Katie's dad. She'd never told us about him, and my parents were scared that if they pushed her, she'd leave. There were a few times in high school that Penny had run away from home. She'd dated this guy in secret—though how she'd managed that one was beyond me.

Even though, now, she wasn't the mess she was growing up, I think that somewhere in the back of my parents' mind, they still worried she'd take off.

And this time, it wasn't just Penny that we would lose, but Katie too.

Not wanting to commit to anything I didn't want to do, I promised Penny that I would think about it and hung up.

And think about it I did. It freaked me out because if this was all fake, then why was he acting depressed enough that Penny picked up on it. If she, with her limited time in the house, had recognized something in him, then the rest of my family must have seen it too. Which made *me* the heartbreaker.

Of course, he could be playing to their sympathies.

I shook my head. Jaxson wasn't like that.

I turned in my seat so I could give Suzie a pleading look. "You have to go get Katie. If I see him, I'll crumble."

She eyed me for a brief second before focusing on the road. "Agreed."

"Hey!" I smacked her arm. "You could have at least let me believe you were thinking about it."

She shrugged as she turned into our drive. I sank low in the seat in case someone was watching out the window. The whole time she was inside, I chewed my lip, alternately praying that Jaxson would come outside and that I wouldn't see him at all.

When Suzie got into the car, she must have seen the desperate look in my eye because she sighed and said, "He wasn't there. Apparently, he's at the gym."

I slouched even further down in my seat.

The ride to the mall was filled with Katie talking and singing. Bless her internal happiness meter—it was hard to stay sad when she covered you with sunshine. By the time we piled out of the car, my mood had risen.

We got inside the mall and stopped at those kiddie rides that they placed right at the entrance to suck in all the kids and parents. Katie rode every one while Suzie and I chatted about everything but Jaxson. We mapped out a plan. There was one great dress shop and two shoe stores to hit. I needed a new moisturizer, so we had to go to the department store too.

Once Katie was done with the rides, I took her hand and we headed to Tulie's Formal Dress Emporium. We spent the next two hours trying on dresses and giggling. It was nice, worrying about something other than my relationship—or lack thereof—with Jaxson for a while. Since we'd broken up, I didn't need to worry about paparazzi showing up and the next headline or meme that would smear my face across the digital world.

Without Jaxson in my life, I was plain old Charlotte again. It was a relief—sort of.

I hadn't realized how special it made me feel to be his fake girl-friend. Not in the surface way of being able to brag about it on social media—which I had never done. But knowing that he was there for me—that if my car had a flat tire, I had a guy to call who would show up. Or, if I fell on the dance floor, he'd scoop me in his arms and rush me to safety. There was a certain kind of connection there, a safety, a bond, and I missed it terribly. I missed him.

But this was for the best.

Like I'd said, loving a man who only pretended to love me was crushing. For my survival, I had to be alone right now.

I stepped out of the changing room and twirled in front of the mirror. The hem of my navy-blue mermaid dress spun out around my calves. I loved the off-the-shoulder sleeves and the V-neck that plunged ever so slightly.

I pulled my hair up and off my shoulders and then turned to Suzie and Katie.

"I think this is the one," I said as I waited for their reaction.

Suzie glanced up from where she was securing a veil on Katie's head and nodded. "Yeah, that's definitely the one."

"You wook like a pwincess," Katie breathed. She stepped up to the mirror and stared at my reflection, taking in the beadwork that swirled across the bodice and down the side of the dress.

With her standing next to me, I looked like the maid of honor to a tiny bride. The image made me laugh.

"Do you think I should get it?" I asked as I crouched down and wrapped my arms around my niece.

Katie nodded, her face was so serious under the gauzy fabric.

I smiled as I stood and glanced back at Suzie. Just as I did, someone passed by the window in the front of the store. I paused. For a ridiculous moment, I allowed myself to think that it was Jaxson. But as my eyes focused, and my mind connected the dots, I realized that it was Jeff Dearden.

He must have felt my stare because he glanced my way. His eyebrows rose as his gaze swept over me. My entire body heated from his appreciative look.

Would Jaxson think the same?

I couldn't think like that. I had to start getting him out of my system if there was ever any hope of moving forward in life. I wasn't even thinking about dating again. I just meant getting up tomorrow and taking another shower, going to the fundraiser, and putting on a McKnight smile.

My stomach sank.

I couldn't do this.

Jeff waved, the movement grabbing my attention.

Maybe, if I had someone to lean on…

I waved Jeff in before I could think this through too far. His forehead wrinkled for a moment before he nodded and came into the store.

"Hey," I said as I walked past the mannequins dressed for an evening out.

Jeff glanced over at Katie and Suzie and then back to me. "How's it going, ladies?"

I lifted my hands. "It's good. We're dress shopping for the hospital fundraiser. Are you going?" I was rushing this but I didn't care. If I didn't make it happen soon, I'd lose my nerve.

Jeff shoved his hands into the front pocket of his jeans and nodded. "I'm thinking about it."

"Do you need a date? 'Cause I need a date." The words tumbled from my lips.

He widened his eyes. "What happened to Jagger? You two have been the hot item for weeks now. It's all over social media."

Was it my imagination or did he just glance at my stomach? I should buy a tee shirt that says "I'm not pregnant" and wear that to the fundraiser. I swallowed as heat permeated my cheeks. "They're all lies. Don't believe any of it." My voice cracked and he reached out to touch my arm in consolation.

"Lottie?"

"I'm good. Really. I just don't want to go alone." I spoke quietly, ashamed that this much emotion was getting through my walls.

Jeff nodded. He got it. I could see him accept that I wasn't interested in him as a potential boyfriend but that I valued the friendship we'd had over the years. He not only accepted it, he echoed it. Which made me feel so much better on so many levels.

Suzie appeared next to Jeff and met my gaze with a warning one of her own. Her eyes said, *slow down, think this through*. "Whatcha doing?" she asked.

"Jeff and I are going to the fundraiser together." I smiled as big as I could.

Suzie stared daggers in Jeff's direction. "Oh really?"

Jeff cleared his throat and nodded. "Just as friends. After all, no need to go alone."

I nodded, feeling more and more confident that this choice was the right one. I would go to the fundraiser, show my family and Jaxson that I was okay, and eventually, everyone would forget about our ridiculous little fake-dating scheme.

Everyone except me. I had a Jaxson tattoo on my heart that wasn't ever going away.

Jaxson would move back to Austin and I would stay here with my broken heart and no one would be any wiser.

If I wanted to prove that I was a strong woman who could love a man like Jaxson and leave him, then going with Jeff was my best option. It sent waves of information out to the world.

If I saw Jaxson again, single and alone, I was pretty sure I'd break.

At least Jeff could prop me up.

After all, what other choice did I have?

16

JAXSON

I'd practically lived at the gym for the last 24 hours.

After Lottie informed me that my mother was staying at the McKnight mansion and that we were breaking up, I really didn't have a desire to head home anytime soon.

It didn't help that I couldn't think about her walking out on me without a huge rock sitting on my chest. Or the fact that my mother might be the reason behind it. So I chose to ignore both situations in true Jagger fashion.

Once it was apparent that Lottie wasn't coming back, I headed right for the gym and worked out until my body was numb and I was too tired to lift. I showered there and snuck into the house.

The next morning, I was up before anyone else stirred. I thought I'd have the kitchen to myself, but just as I walked into the kitchen, Penny spotted me, making my retreat impossible.

"Morning," she'd said over the rim of her steaming mug.

I ducked my head, worried my pain would be written across my forehead in black ink. "Yep." Yep? I wasn't functioning on normal levels, so I tried again. "You're up early."

"You too," she fired back. "I didn't see Lottie come in—were you guys out late?"

The implication in her voice caused a stab of pain in my heart. I wish we'd been out late doing the things Penny thought we shouldn't do.

"No, we, uh, broke up." I hurriedly opened the cereal cupboard and stuck my face in to hide the burn that spread across my skin. "You know—fake broke up. We aren't doing the pretend relationship anymore." I did my best to emphasize the word "pretend" without sounding like I was trying too hard. Man, I was such a spaz.

"Oh."

I tried to read something into her reply but I couldn't, it was too small. My shoulders rounded as I considered my breakfast options and avoided turning around.

"Jaxson?"

I steeled myself. I had to answer her now. "Yeah?" I casually looked over my shoulder.

"Is everything all right?"

No. Nothing was right. And it wouldn't ever be again. I'd screwed up my chance with Lottie. "It's great." I shut the cupboard and walked quickly across the room, intent on getting out of there. "We're out of protein bars. I'm going to pick some up on my way to the gym."

"Oh, okay. Bye," she called behind me.

Hours of mindless wandering around town passed, and I still hadn't eaten anything.

Lottie hadn't called, and I could only assume that meant she hadn't come home as well. My mom texted a few times, but I ignored her.

Yet again, she was the reason for my broken heart. As much as I hated that I was treating her this way, she'd been the one to leave first. Lottie had been a breath of fresh air in my life, and she'd chased that happiness away too.

I wasn't quite ready to hug and sing" Kumbaya" anytime soon.

I rushed into the McKnight mansion later that evening after a grueling session at the gym. I had my gym bag in tow, and I was ready to hunker down for the night. I was going to make my excuses for not going to the fundraiser to Liam and barricade myself in my room.

Liam stood in front of his mirror, adjusting his tie. I rapped on the open door.

He glanced my way and then did a double take. "Dude, you cannot wear those shorts to the dinner. My mom will kill you."

I shook my head. "I'm not going."

"What? Why not?" He strode to his bed and picked up the tuxedo jacket lying there.

"The mayor basically fired me. Some big-shot actor is going to emcee. I think showing up would make me look pathetic."

"Or like a total stud for supporting the hospital even after the mayor pulled a jerk-move." He slid his arms into the jacket and tugged it on. "Besides, you'll disappoint my parents if you don't come. Mason is getting a community award tonight for rescuing that little boy."

Well, shoot.

Liam stopped and really gave me a once over. "You look like crap."

"I know. I'll shower. Give me twenty min—"

"No. I mean, you look like *crap*." He stepped closer and stared at my face. "Your mom's been worried about you, and I'm starting to see why."

"You've talked to her?" I asked, hating the fact that my voice sounded weak when I mentioned Mrs. Jagger.

I used to be strong. That was before Lottie tore down all my defenses. Now, all that was left of me was this sniveling man who couldn't seem to get his life together.

"What do you think? She came all this way to see you and you've been MIA. I know she's trying to be strong, but she's pretty broken. Plus, she keeps going on and on about a baby?"

My heart stuttered to a stop as I stared at Liam. I could only imagine what he would do to me if he realized people actually thought I'd impregnated his sister.

His skin remained the same color, and he continued talking as if he didn't care. "I didn't know one of your siblings is expecting." He reached out and clapped me on the shoulders. "Congrats, uncle."

Crap

"Um, they aren't," I said slowly. "None of my siblings are pregnant. I don't even think any of them are seriously dating."

Liam slowed his movements until he was just standing there, staring at the ground. Then he tipped his head ever so slightly to the side, and I could see the realization in his gaze.

"I should kill you," he said in a low voice.

I lifted both my arms weakly. "Go ahead." If I was honest with myself, I wanted to kill me too. I'd failed at everything. I'd become the man my father always assumed I would be.

His chin jerked back. "It's one thing to fake-date my sister, but to have the world think that you..." He paused and closed his eyes as his jaw muscles flinched. I'd been on the receiving end of his wrath before. I knew what was coming.

"She dumped me. Last night." I scrubbed my face. "It's over. I'll have Brent run a press release, and all the confusion will be cleared up."

He paused and studied me. But he didn't look relieved. Instead, his gaze hardened. "I'm starting to think your crappy look has nothing to do with your mom thinking you're having a baby and a lot to do with Lottie dumping you."

I was tired of all of this faking. Lottie was right, it only hurt the people we cared about. So I offered a small shrug and I saw his expression turn to one of pure rage.

He knew.

I'd done the one thing I promised him I wouldn't do.

I'd fallen for Lottie.

He grabbed the front of my shirt. "What is wrong with you?"

"I don't know." I slumped. "I fell in love with her and she walked."

He shoved me away. "*You* fell in love with my baby sister? The girl who used to sit between us on the couch with a tub of popcorn."

A grin tugged at the corners of my mouth at the memory. She was so tiny back then. Okay, maybe she wasn't that small, but she'd felt so much younger than us, just like a little sister. She didn't feel that way anymore. She was still five-foot-five but she was all woman, delicate and graceful. Well, when she wasn't dancing.

"I'm sorry, man. It was a bonehead move, I know. You told me not to…" I ran my hand down my face.

"When?" he demanded.

I thought back. "That first day home. She made me make my own bed."

He snorted in disgust, and I realized "bed" and "baby sister" were a bad combo in his mind. "It was before I knew who she was—when I thought she was the nanny. For some reason, I didn't see your baby sister, I just saw her."

He paced the room. "You're an idiot."

"Yeah. I figured that out all on my own. Thanks."

He stopped and stared up at the ceiling, like the next question was difficult to spit out. "Does she love you back?" He might as well have been asking a mechanic: How much is the repair going to cost me? For all the emotions packed in there.

I sank onto his bed. "She said she did."

He cuffed the back of my head. "Then get up."

I jumped up, rubbing my sore spot and getting out of his personal space. "What the heck?"

Liam stepped toe-to-toe with me and shoved my shoulder. "I don't know what went down, but if she's actually in love with you while you're sitting here moping, I'm going to kill you."

"But—" What was happening here?

"Listen. I don't like the thought of you guys *together*." He shuddered. "But if you mess this up and hurt her—then you're out of the family."

"But I don't even know where she is. And do you have permission to just kick me out?"

His eyebrows rose at the question, so I decided to stop talking.

He roughly shoved me toward the door—both hands this time. "You know where she'll be."

His words lit a fire under me. I spun and grabbed both his arms and brought him in for a massive bro hug. He pounded me once on the back, hard. I got the feeling he was struggling a lot more than he let on. "I'm sorry," I mumbled, hating the surge of emotion that coursed through me.

I'd gone from feeling very much alone, to feeling cared about in one swoop.

"What for?" Liam asked as he pulled back.

"For not trusting you more as a brother." I hadn't thought he'd have my back—or Lottie's—in this way. I'd thought telling him how I felt about his sister would be the end of our friendship. I'd judged him with the same yardstick I'd grown up with and forgotten that he was a McKnight—and that meant something when it came to loyalty.

"Dude. Shut up and take a shower," he replied with a grin and a punch to the shoulder.

I didn't respond. Instead, I sprinted up the stairs like I hadn't just run twenty miles on the treadmill to forget the woman I love. I careened into my bedroom, grabbing the doorjamb to keep me from flying into the bed, and stopped short.

My mom was sitting in the chair in the corner.

I cursed under my breath. "Hi."

She stood, smoothing down her formal gown. Wonderful. She was going to the fundraiser. That wasn't going to make things awkward. "I'm kind of in a hurry." I pulled off my shirt and threw it in the hamper as a nudge to get her out of the room.

"I haven't seen you since I got here." She clasped her hands in front of her and looked down at them.

"If I'd known you were coming"—and going to wreak havoc on my love life—"I would have scheduled some time for you." Lie. Lie. Lie. Okay, maybe not a full fabrication. I would have gone out to dinner with her. I just wouldn't have lived under the same roof. The McKnights were way nicer people than I was.

Speaking of lies. "Lottie isn't pregnant."

Mom's head came up. "But—"

"I know you talked to her yesterday. She said you were so excited she couldn't break your heart and tell you she wasn't carrying your grandchild."

"But you can?" she whispered.

I bit back my first, snarky, response. Something in her voice—a level of pain I'd never heard before, caught me. "It's not that. You need to know the truth. Those articles...they make stuff up to sell advertising space."

Mom looked confused but then she slowly nodded.

"I can give you the blanket back." My mind jumped back to watching Lottie stuff it in her purse. I'd have to ask her for it. I would ask her; that would be a great way to tell her I'd explained everything to Mom. Just like she wanted me to.

Mom's shoulders began to shake.

I stared. "Are you...crying?"

She sniffed and swiped at her eyes. "No."

"Jaggers don't cry," I repeated out of training.

She garbled a response.

I looked up for a moment and then I threw my shirt back on and went over to give her a hug. It was what Lottie would have done. She must be rubbing off on me. Either that, or love was making me a softie. "Mom, you'll have grandkids one day." I rubbed her back.

She laugh-cried into my chest. "I want my son back."

Oh boy. I glanced at the clock on the nightstand. "Mom, I'd love to clear twenty-some-odd years of air, but I have a thing. And Lottie is going to be at that thing. And this may be my best shot at getting her back."

"Back?" Mom pushed out of my hold. "Jaxson Dylan Jagger, what have you done?"

"All the wrong things." I looked pointedly at the clock. "And if I don't shower before setting them right, Lottie will smell me coming a mile away."

She looked down at my clothes and tugged an invisible piece of lint off my shirt. "She's a good one, Jax. I remember when we lived here, she volunteered at the elementary school on Wednesday afternoons. She's the reason Ryan started reading so well. I think he had a little crush on her."

We'd moved around a lot with my dad in the military. Three times in three years before we landed in Evergreen Hollow. Ryan got further and further behind in his reading level. Mom did her best, but he was angry. He'd just get settled in and then lose all his friends and have to start over. "Nothing like a beautiful set of blue eyes to give a man motivation." I smiled. "Ryan always did like blondes."

"You like her too?" Mom ventured.

"I love her." I said the words as simply and as easily as if they were a fact I'd known my whole life. Like saying the sky is blue or water is wet.

Mom's hands covered her mouth and her eyes filled with tears.

I wasn't comfortable with this new revelation that my mother cried. She's always pressed her lips together and gotten through. "Mom. Come on."

She laughed. "I'm just so… To hear you say those words so openly." She fanned her face. I thought back to my childhood. I couldn't remember hearing my dad tell Mom he loved her—or any of us. What a sad way for a woman to live. I would never do that to Lottie. She was going to hear "I love you" until she was sick of it.

If I could ever get to the event and tell her.

"Jax." Liam appeared in the doorway. "We're leaving."

I glanced at my mom. "I'll drive myself."

"No," Mom made her way to the door. "I'll drive you over in my rental. That way, you can drive home with Lottie after you kiss and make up."

Liam blanched.

"I'll take that ride." I ushered the two of them out the door, grabbed the handle, and shut it tight. I stepped back, expecting it to open again. When it didn't, I made a mad dash for the shower.

I was going to tell Lottie I loved her and that I wanted to be her everything.

But I'd settle for being her *real* boyfriend.

Everything else could come later.

I glanced at myself in the mirror and then my eyes hit on the tube of green paint on the counter. The one I'd used to become the Hulk. An idea about how I could reach Lottie started to form.

I pulled out my phone and called the mayor as I disrobed.

"Mayor Thomas's phone, this is his assistant speaking."

Perfect. "Hi, this is Jaxson Jagger. I was supposed to emcee tonight, but that seems to have fallen through. My agent is pretty upset, he'd already done a blurb or two about the event."

"Oh. Um…" She was flustered, which was perfect for me.

"I'm hoping the mayor will want to make it up to me."

"Can you hold?"

"No. I'm running late. Listen, why don't we do a little stage time, maybe after Sheriff McKnight gets his award." I thought fast. "He's an old family friend, and I'd like to congratulate him."

"I'm absolutely positive we can make that happen." I could feel her relief through the phone.

"Perfect. I'll be there. I have something special planned." I studied the body paint.

"I've already added you to the program."

"You're amazing. Tell the mayor I said so."

"Thank you very much."

We said goodbye and hung up. I jumped into the shower and I grinned as the water hit me right in the face. No matter what Lottie said—no matter if she took my heart out and stomped on it in front of a couple hundred people—I was going to say all the things I should have said from the beginning.

Hopefully she'd kiss me.

But she'd probably punch me first.

I was good with that.

17

LOTTIE

I scanned the assembly hall for any sign of Jaxson the moment I walked into the room.

I didn't see him, and my entire body felt as if it were crashing. I let out the breath I was holding. My nerves were in a jumble worse than grandma's knitting yarn after the cat got into it.

Jeff patted my hand that rested in the crook of his arm. "The room is nice."

Nice was an understatement. The assembly hall had been transformed into an art studio. Children's artwork was on display around the room in the silent auction. A few local artists had also donated pieces, which, from where I stood, were quite striking. But I preferred the primary colors and broad strokes of hope the children painted.

"Is your dad coming?" Jeff spoke, drawing my attention over to him.

"Of course." I watched him for a minute. "Why? Are you nervous?"

He sighed heavily. "Confession? I wanted to ask him to be my partner in the expansion project." He glanced down, sheepish. "It's not the reason I came with you tonight, though. I'm glad we're here—as friends."

Ah. Things were starting to make sense. There had been no—read it zero—attraction between the two of us. His sudden interest in me at Carter's party and then his willingness to go along with my charade had seemed strange. Knowing that he wanted access to my father—well, it made me feel better about using him to get back at Jaxson.

Sure, this wasn't my finest moment, but at least I wasn't the only one mooching off the other. We both had an agenda, and we both knew what the other one was doing.

Win-win.

I smiled. "Me too." I looked around and picked out my dad amongst my brothers. They were all congregated around the refreshment table. Typical. "Listen, why don't you make your pitch before he knows you came with me. Then you won't have to wonder if he said yes—or no—because you went out with me—as friends." I smiled easily to let him know I was teasing him with the last comment.

"I don't want to leave you alone. That wouldn't be gentlemanly." He swallowed and I saw a flash of fear in his gaze. I tried not to roll my eyes. It was the same look every guy got when it came to my brothers and me. To be completely honest, I was getting quite tired of it.

I nodded and shot him a dazzling smile. "I won't be alone. Suzie is right there."

He glanced quickly in her direction. A spark of worry lit up his face, making me chuckle inside. "Go. I'll meet you at the table for dinner."

"Thanks" He patted my hand once more before adjusting his tie and striding purposefully after my dad.

I looked for Jaxson once more.

"Stop." Suzie put her hand on my arm as she joined me. "He's not here."

Heat raced to my cheeks and I began shaking my head like a dog after a bath. "I'm not looking, you're looking."

Great. Real mature, Charlotte.

Suzie raised her eyebrows and I could see "crazy person" flash through her eyes. I sighed and shrugged as I swallowed, my mouth suddenly turning dry.

Man, I was anxious. Suddenly, coming here felt like a horrible idea.

Suzie continued to stare at me like she was a moment away from admitting me into a loony bin—with a brother that is a doctor and a sister that's a nurse, that wouldn't be too hard.

"I can't help it." I tugged on the zipper of my clutch. It was gold to match my shoes, which looked stunning with the mermaid dress.

"Can't help what?" asked Penny, coming up behind us and holding tight to Katie's hand. Penny was a showstopper in a black high-panel, V-neck dress. The bodice was covered in gold lace and the hem scalloped with the same.

"You look awesome!" I exclaimed.

She laughed and patted her hair. She had a thick braid that went from her part on the left side and then over to the right, secured seamlessly into her barrel curls. "A little different from scrubs, huh?"

I hated to say it, so I didn't, but I'd forgotten how beautiful my sister was. I hugged her lightly. "You're stunning."

She squeezed me in thanks.

Meanwhile, Suzie was making a fuss over Katie's outfit. Her dress was green with a white, shimmery overlay and pearl beading on the bodice. Her hair was also curled and had a twist around the crown of her head.

"I'm so glad you came." I bent down and hugged her.

She positively beamed. "Dis is my pwincess dress."

"And you're a princess in it." I tapped her nose.

Penny glanced around. "I'm not sure how long we'll stay. She can't sit still long." If Mason wasn't getting an award, Penny wouldn't have brought Katie along. But this was a big deal, and we McKnights stuck together as a family. It was in our DNA.

"She's about the age we were when we started coming to these things." I stood up and smoothed out my dress.

Penny rolled her eyes. "I can't imagine what Mom was thinking dragging a brood like us to formal dinners."

"I was thinking that I loved my kids." But when we both gave her a *sure you did* look, she laughed and shrugged. "Okay, so I didn't want to leave you home to tear the place apart." Mom came up behind us and put one arm around each of us. "You girls look lovely."

Before we could even say thank you, Ashley, the assistant volunteer coordinator over the children's cancer floor approached with her hand out. "It's good to see you again," she said.

I made quick introductions. The longer I was there, talking with people and acting normal, the easier it became to pretend that things were normal. Suzie excused herself and took Katie to the dance floor. There was a band playing music softly, and Katie wanted to test her new shoes. I was surprised that Penny had loosened up enough to allow Katie to wear a heel.

"Where's Jaxson?" Ashley asked looking around.

"He's emceeing tonight," I said by way of excusing him without explaining anything.

"Didn't you hear?" Mom said. "They changed out the emcee at the last minute."

"They did?" My heart rate picked up. I hoped I hadn't ruined the evening for the hospital by chasing Jaxson out of town. That would add a whole ton of guilt on top of my already mixed-up emotions. Plus, that would mean he wasn't here. And I wasn't sure I was ready for him to leave.

"Well, you'll have to tell him later." Ashley waved a hand through the air.

"Tell him what?" I asked.

Ashley bounced on her bright pink toes. "The hospital job is yours." Her smile brightened times five. "I talked to the coordinator today. He's going to call you on Monday with an official offer, but he said I could pass the news along tonight."

Mom wrapped her arm around me and squeezed. "Congratulations, honey."

I blinked in shock. My arms stuck to my sides. I couldn't even raise them to hug my mom back. "I have the job?"

"It's yours for the taking," Ashley confirmed.

The reality of it finally sunk in. I'd gotten a job—without Jaxson's help. A sense of accomplishment and pride washed over me. *Finally*, I thought. Laughing, I hugged my mom back. "I'm not the screwup." I said the words before I knew what I was saying.

"The what?" Mom asked, confused.

Penny leaned closer.

I did not want to have this conversation in front of Ashley. "Thank you so much for telling me." I ignored Mom's pressing look and turned to hug Ashley too. Thankfully, Mom left us alone while I chatted with my future co-worker. She told me where I would go to fill out paperwork and who I should talk to on Monday, and then she saw someone else she needed to talk to. Like a fairy job-mother she flitted off to bestow her sparkles somewhere else.

The second we were alone, Penny grabbed my hand. "What did you mean you're the screwup?"

A lump formed in the back of my throat. "Can we not talk about this now?" I waved my hand around, indicating the whole evening.

Mom shook her head. "I think we'd better crack open this nut."

I looked up, tears making serious, mob-boss level threats about falling in front of everyone. "I'm so far behind everyone. And when I graduated without a job—and Carter's a full doctor and Mason is saving lives and I was nothing."

Penny yanked me in for a big-sister hug. "You saved me and Katie this summer. I don't know what we would have done without you."

"All I did was babysit."

She looked into my eyes. "All you did was provide a safe place for my daughter. Do you have any idea how much that means to me?"

I lifted a shoulder.

Mom put her hand on my back. "Sweetie, no one thought poorly of you for not having a job. My goodness, we were so happy you were able to come home. I missed you when you were at college. You are my last one and the house was so empty without you." She hugged both me and Penny. "I love you both, and I understand that you have to find your way—just like I did. It takes time, and sometimes the road bends." She touched her forehead to Penny's temple. Of all us kids, Penny's road had the most twists. "But I wouldn't have it any other way, and it doesn't mean you aren't worth rubies."

I nodded, the tears following through with their threats as they tumbled down my cheeks. The music stopped and someone announced that we should take our seats, dinner would be served soon.

Mom let us go and we gathered up Katie and Suzie on our way to the table.

Penny fell back a few steps, taking me with her. "Did you talk to Jaxson?"

I sealed my lips and shook my head. She frowned but dropped the subject as we reached our table and took our seats with the rest of the family.

Jeff appeared, pulling my seat out for me and then helping Penny with hers too.

I lifted an eyebrow, silently asking how his pitch had gone. He gave me a small shrug letting me know the matter was undecided. I was rooting for him though. He was a good person, and I wanted good things for him.

"Where's Liam?" I asked. I figured he and Jaxson would be together, so if I knew where my brother was, I could prepare to see Jaxson too.

"I'm not sure..." Mom smiled as Dad found the table and leaned down to kiss her cheek in greeting.

"Ladies and Gentlemen, Mayor Thomas," said an unknown female voice over the speakers. The mayor took the stage, raising one hand in a political wave as he crossed to the mic. We all clapped politely.

I checked for Jaxson again. Maybe he really wasn't coming.

The mayor grinned. "What a beautiful night." He launched into a speech about the hospital and the need to raise funds for research as well as new equipment and updates. I glassed over, a polite smile on my face while inside I was breaking down fast.

I missed Jaxson.

I missed holding his hand and the way he'd brush his thumb over my knuckle. I missed the sexy way he lifted one side of his mouth to smile before the other joined it. I missed the way every moment felt alive when I was with him.

"Our emcee for the evening…"

I came back to the program, hoping maybe my mom was wrong and Jaxson really was coming out from behind the curtain.

"…Academy Award–winning actor, Chris Hartman."

Penny gasped loudly. She reached out and grabbed my hand, squeezing it tightly. The curtains parted and Chris made his way on stage, his signature swagger making no less than five women squeal. Quite a few more called out that they loved him, and everyone clapped loudly.

My fingers started to tingle. They needed blood. "Penny," I hissed.

She didn't relent. If anything, she squeezed them tighter. Man, my sister had some grip strength.

"Let go." I twisted my hand free and rubbed my knuckles. "What is with you?" I glanced from her to the stage. Her eyes were locked on Chris. I'd had no idea she was such a big fan. I mean the guy made a great superhero, but so did a lot of the Hollywood Chrises.

I'd never seen my sister stare so hard at him before. Sure, he was one of Evergreen Hollow's claims to fame. We were a small town, but we birthed heartthrob Chris Hartman and two NFL players. And trust me, our town used that. A lot.

But we all knew he was a jerk. He'd broken a lot of hearts on his way to the A-list—from the look on my sister's face, she might have been one of them.

And I'd always thought she was the smarter sister.

Dad leaned over, a teasing look in his eye "They're auctioning off dinner with him. Do you want me to put down a bid?"

"No!" Penny snapped, her face dark. We all reared back as if she'd snarled. "I mean, no thanks." She fanned her red face. "I think it was a shock to see him in person again. I thought he was done with our small town." She took a large sip from her ice water, glancing at Katie. "Are you okay, sweetheart? If you're bored, we can go."

Katie was kneeling on her seat so she could see everything on stage. She put her finger over Penny's lips and told her mom to "Shh."

Penny nodded but looked as if she were ready to sprint to the exit at a moment's notice. Man, she was really worked up. I made a mental note to ask her about that later.

Chris talked on and on, and I found my mind wandering. It seemed that I was the one who couldn't hold still. I wanted to sit up and tell him to hurry it along. The more he talked, the longer it was before I saw Jaxson. I was exhausted from the stress of staring over my shoulder at the wide-open double doors to see if he came in late.

All I wanted to do was make sure he was okay. If anything, I was being the one thing we'd agreed on being from the beginning, a friend helping out another friend.

I groaned inwardly.

Who was I kidding? I needed to see him. I was in love with the man and being apart from him was going to drive me crazy. How would I ever survive without another one of his kisses?

I was doomed.

18

JAXSON

I peeked out from behind the curtain, zeroing in on the McKnight table. "What is she doing here with Jeff?" I whispered.

Liam parted the curtains with his fingers. "I don't know. But, dude, he's the least of your worries right now." He snickered as he let the curtains fall shut.

Mason shook his head at me.

"What?" I demanded.

"If you were trying to prove that you really love her, this did it." He waved his hand up and down, motioning toward my Hulk look.

I looked down at my bare torso, now covered in green body paint. "Maybe this is a bad idea."

"You can't back out now," whisper-wailed Demi, the mayor's assistant. "I have you in the program as 'Surprise Guest.' Any second now, Chris is going to present the award to Mason and then you're up."

"Sheriff McKnight!" said Chris at that very moment.

"Oh, for the love of Pete," Mason marched on stage like a man marching to the gallows.

Liam and I hung back in the shadows.

"He loves this stuff, doesn't he?" I joked. I needed to take my mind off my own set of nerves, and focusing on Mason seemed to help. Liam blew a raspberry. "He'd rather pull his toenails off."

Mason stood there for a moment while Chris recounted his heroic action in saving Grayson. Images flashed of the accident and the charred car shone on a screen off to the right. A moment later, Grayson and Sadie joined him on stage. Sadie stood as far off to the side as she could.

"Great," muttered Liam.

"What?" I glanced back and forth between the stage and him.

"I didn't realize the kid was Sadie's."

"No way," I whispered as I turned back to look closer at the woman on stage. "Seriously? Sadie, as in *that* Sadie?"

"Yeah. It's her. I'll bet Mason is hating this."

"What really happened there?" All I'd ever heard were rumors.

Liam lifted a shoulder. "Mason hasn't told me the whole story. There's bad blood—that's for sure."

Weird. "And he saved her kid's life. It looks like she can barely stand him—even after that."

Sadie and her son left the stage going one direction, and Mason headed the other to join his family at their table—toting a glass award proclaiming him a real-life hero.

"You're up." Liam started pushing me toward the stage.

"Hey, slow down." My heart pounded so loudly in my ears, I couldn't hear Chris's introduction. I couldn't hear anything. Liam parted the curtain and gave me a final push, his laughter echoing loudly.

I hoped he got green paint all over his hand.

Jerk.

My arrival in the spotlights brought on a round of applause and more than a little laughter. I flushed with heat and prayed the makeup wouldn't melt. I lumbered to the middle of the stage as Chris waved me over. He was a good sport to do this on such short notice.

"Hulk, buddy. Glad to see you." He went to shake my hand and then backed off. I was doing my best to stay in character, holding my arms out away from my body and sneering.

"What's the matter big guy?"

Chris put the mic in front of my mouth.

"Hulk sad," I replied. The longer I was up here, the more stupid I felt. I couldn't see Lottie. The spotlights made it hard to see past the first row of tables.

"Why's that?" Christ stuck to the script.

"Hulk miss Lottie." Oh my gosh, this was the dumbest thing I'd ever done in my life. I could hear Liam rolling behind the stage.

But I was in this for the million-dollar payoff of having the woman I loved in my arms, so I was going full-send. "Hulk love Lottie. Hulk sorry."

The lights changed, moving one spotlight onto the McKnight family table. It was just enough to allow me to see her. Her face was pale, but she was as beautiful as ever.

I slightly melted under her stare. She wasn't smiling. She wasn't laughing. She was mad.

I swallowed, wishing I had never done this. I was an idiot. An idiot with a broken heart.

"Hulk want forgiveness," I whispered as I watched Lottie stand and storm out. "Lottie!" I called after her, thankfully finding enough strength to speak.

She didn't slow. Instead, she picked up her skirt and took off.

"Go after her," the crowd yelled at me. Apparently, everyone was invested.

I stared at the direction she'd gone for a moment and then over to Jeff, who was now standing and waving his arms like an air traffic controller for me to go after his date.

The crowd began to chant and that bolstered me. I'd watched her walk away once, there was no way on this green earth I was going to do it again.

I jumped from the stage, earning myself a roar of applause. If things were going according to plan, I would have raised my fists above my head and roared. But Lottie was awfully fast for someone wearing such a tight dress.

I dropped the whole Hulk act and sprinted, my bare feet slapping against the wooden floor. The whole room was in an uproar as I cleared the doors and made it to the lobby.

Lottie was almost to the exit. I had to do something. In an act of desperation, I called out, "Lottie—stop!"

19

LOTTIE

I spun on Jaxson, madder than a…a…red hen. Whatever that meant. What was he thinking? Of all the idiotic ways to apologize, he chose doing it in a Hulk costume in front of my family and new boss? Was he serious?

I stopped, my anger freezing me at the door. I wanted to push through, but I couldn't. It was like my legs were made of lead.

Jaxson got the wrong idea as he rushed to me, his arms open.

I glared at him, and just when he was in reach, I punched him right in the gut.

He winced, but that didn't stop him.

"You stupid jerk," I yelled as I cradled my wrist. My knuckles were covered in green and my hand throbbed. I hated it, but the thought of his abs flashed in my mind.

"I'm sorry." He reached for my hand. "Did I hurt you?"

If he only knew.

All of my emotions bubbled over, and a laugh burst out like the sound of a balloon popping. Tears followed close behind. "Yes, you hurt me. Why do you have such a hard stomach?" I studied my hand. There didn't seem to be any damage. I'd jammed my wrist was all. It stung, but I would survive. I shook it out and glared up at him.

He furrowed his brow in concern, which only made me more mad. How could he be so adorable? It wasn't fair. How was a woman supposed to resist a man when he knowingly made a fool of himself for her? The makeup, the voice? It was too much for me to handle.

Add the flashbacks to the supply closet that made the butterflies in my stomach lift off, and I was slowly losing my will to stay angry. I swallowed down my emotions and glared up at him. Emotions were ridiculous things, and I was beginning to see them as useless.

"Why are you running away from me?" He stepped closer. Even with all that body paint on, he smelled like he'd just stepped out of the shower.

"Because, you're using me again." The anger that had filled me with the energy to outrun him returned. "I told you, I can't lie anymore. I can't pretend."

He shook his head. "I'm not pretending."

I leveled a look at him. "The stage makeup says otherwise."

He threw his hands up. "Okay, so that was a bad idea. I thought it would be romantic—bring up good memories."

"Of what? Your other publicity stunt?"

"No." He reached for me and adjusted his hands so they only touched the parts of my arms that the dress didn't and held on. His fingers were firm and soft, and just having that much contact send a pleasant buzzing through my traitorous body. I wanted to hate him so much. It would be easier than loving him as much as I did.

"What happened in that closet wasn't pretend," he said. His voice dropped an octave. A warm rush of feeling washed over me. He leaned closer all the while, keeping his gaze on me. If I were ice, I'd be a puddle of water right now.

I slowly shook my head. I couldn't believe him. It was too scary and overwhelming to wrap my head around. Everything had been pretend for him, right? For me, it felt as real as the ground under my feet or the breeze on my face. Loving Jaxson came as easy as breathing.

I just felt. That was it. I didn't need any reason or explanation. I was born to love him.

"When I kissed you on the football field, I felt something change inside of me." He ducked so I'd meet his eyes. "It was the same feeling as when I kissed you at my graduation party."

I blinked a few times as tears formed on my eyelids. I didn't want to cry; I wanted to be strong. But everything he said hit me like I'd never imagined the truth would hit me. "You remember?"

He moved to hold me close, but shook his head. He muttered something about "dumb paint" and kept his distance. "You had on a light-blue dress and cherry Chapstick." He took my hand and kissed it. "And you changed me that night. You made me see something inside of myself that I've been trying to live up to ever since. You made me believe I was worth something. You make me face the demons of my past."

I used my free hand to cup his cheek, not caring if my entire body was smeared in paint. Touching Jaxson was worth it. He had to know that. "You are worth it," I whispered, but it felt hollow. If I'd learned something over these last few days, it was that words could be spoken, truth or lies. What mattered was action.

He shook his head. "Because of you, Lottie. I love you." He closed his eyes and pressed his forehead to mine. "I want to prove it's true."

"Then why the big show?" I asked.

His eyes flew open. "I was trying for a big romantic gesture."

I shook my head. Silly boy. "I don't need all this." I traced my finger along his green jaw. "I just need to hear you say it."

He laced our fingers together and brought my body within a breath of his. I was dying to be held in his arms, and he was being so careful with my dress, it was killing me. "I love you," he whispered, our lips barely touching.

With a moan, I threw myself into his arms. He caught me, a look of surprise on his face. "But—'"

I silenced him with my lips. I didn't want to hear the reasons we shouldn't be together, shouldn't kiss, or shouldn't be in love. Or even that he shouldn't smear my dress with his green paint. Because this is what I wanted more than anything—him.

All of him.

He picked me up, and a moment later I felt the door at my back. I didn't let go. I didn't break the kiss. Maybe I feared he'd take back everything he'd said. That somehow this was a dream and I was going to wake up. He pressed the bar and the door released. A moment later, we were in the parking lot, the summer heat sticking to our skin.

"Where's your car?" he asked through our lips.

I waved in the direction I hoped was east.

He scooped up my legs and headed that way without hardly breaking our lips apart. I could not get enough of him. He set me on the trunk and cupped my face. "You're a mess." He nuzzled my nose, no doubt covering my nose with green paint.

I laughed. "You're one to talk."

"Ahem!"

We turned to find Mason standing there with my clutch.

"I could arrest you for having your hands all over my sister—but the green paint says you've been keeping it PG."

I glanced down and, sure enough, there were handprints on my sides and arms. "This is my first time being busted by a cop." I leaned my head against Jaxson's shoulder and smiled at Mason.

"Let's make sure it's your only time." Mason held out my clutch. "I assume your keys are in here."

I nodded. "Thanks."

He turned to Jaxson. "You treat her right, or I will make you sleep in a cell."

Jaxson nodded. "You'll never have a reason."

"Good thing." Mason dipped his head and headed back inside. Just before he rounded the corner and disappeared, he turned his head. I followed his gaze to a woman and her son who were hurrying to their car.

"Isn't that...?" I cut off quickly. Sadie was a sore subject around Mason, though I didn't exactly know why.

"I'll see you guys at home," Mason called as he headed back inside. "Remember, Jagger, I'm always watching."

I turned to Jaxson, who saluted Mason, ready to focus on just him.

I giggled as I wrapped my arms around his neck and pulled him close. "Well, Mr. Jagger. It looks like it's just you and me."

"Finally," he breathed. "Be mine, Lottie. No pretending. No fake girlfriend stuff. I just want to be with you."

I moved in to kiss him but stopped. "Your mom." I swallowed.

Jaxson growled as he pulled back to look at me. "Don't bring up a dude's mom right before he kisses you."

I smiled as I ran my fingers through his hair. "We have to tell her."

He raised his eyebrows. "We do?"

I nodded. "Yeah. She's going to be surprised if a baby doesn't appear in nine months."

Jaxson's smile turned into a devious one as he leaned in. "Well…"

I smacked his arm. "Jaxson Jagger, I swear."

Jaxson chuckled as he pulled me close. "I already talked to her. She knows everything." He pressed his lips to the tip of my nose. "But don't disregard our baby so fast. It's something you should get used to."

My heart fluttered as I stared at Jaxson. My entire body flooded with feelings for him. Deep, abiding feelings that I'd never felt for anyone and never wanted to stop feeling for him.

"Our baby?" I asked, the word sounding so foreign yet thrilling on my tongue.

He steeled his gaze as he studied me. "Someday. I love you, Lottie. I can't imagine myself with anyone else."

The future seemed scary, but I knew one thing was for sure. If I had Jaxson by my side, I could do anything. I was never letting him go.

"I love you, too." I kissed him lightly. I finally had Jaxson Jagger all to myself, and I wasn't about to let him go.

EPILOGUE

PENNY

$\mathcal{H}$e was here.

Chris—for the love of Pete—Hartman was here.

As much as I tried to ignore it, I could feel his presence in the room. I sensed his gaze on me—on Katie—as I tried to keep up with the conversation going on around me.

Heat pricked at my spine as my stomach flip-flopped for the millionth time since he walked onto that stage and back into my life.

I peeked at my family. Thankfully, no one had picked up on my anxiety. They'd been distracted by Jaxson and Lottie's big exit. I knew they were in love—they'd been too miserable apart to be anything but totally and completely head over heels for one another.

Dad said something that had Mason and Carter chortling. They talked as if nothing earth-shattering was happening right in front of them. If they only knew.

Dad had even teased me about bidding on the date night with Chris like I was some fan who was dazzled by his stardom.

Which is how I wanted it.

No one needed to know about the tornado going on inside of me. No one needed to know how craptastic it was that Chris was back in town—and from the looks of it, the time away from here had done him good.

Why did he have to look more handsome and put together than when he ran out on me four, er, five years ago?

Why couldn't he have gotten shorter and fatter and maybe developed a mole growing hair on his forehead?

I swallowed my frustration and grabbed Katie's hand. If I hung around here any longer, I was going to explode. And I was pretty sure my parents would notice a giant pile of goo where I once sat.

"Come on," I mumbled as I practically pulled Katie to her feet.

Jaxson and Lottie had rushed off somewhere. Mason had accepted his award. And the mayor was standing next to Chris, wrapping up the evening's festivities. I'd fulfilled my duty to my family and was free to go.

If I ducked out of here right now, I'd miss the end-of-the-evening traffic—and any chance encounter with Chris that was likely to happen if I stayed.

"I'm taking Katie home." I threw the words over my shoulder as I hurried from the table. I wasn't sure if Mom responded or not. Anything she might have said was drowned out by Katie's wails about leaving early mixed with the band's opening chords.

I was half dragging Katie from the room. I'm sure I looked like a crazed person. I could feel my braid coming loose, and I was pretty sure in my acrobatic attempt to pull Katie up onto my hip, I popped a seam.

I was a woman on a mission, and I was leaving the assembly hall if it was the last thing I did.

"Penny?"

That familiar, syrupy-sweet voice stopped me in my tracks just outside the double doors. Katie squirmed and complained, and my mind screamed at my body to keep moving, but I didn't. I just stood there like an idiot.

How could he still have this effect on me even after all these years? Even after he broke my heart?

Why wasn't I stronger? Smarter?

I didn't move, but that didn't stop Chris from moving to stand in front of me. His rich brown eyes stared back at me. His hand was extended as if that was all it would take to get me to forgive him. "Wow, it's been a long time."

I pinched my lips together and nodded. I didn't want to speak. I didn't want to give anything away. I was finally comfortable with my life, with Katie, and with my job as a caretaker for—of course—his grandmother.

I'd taken the position before I knew he was returning. I loved his grandma, she was an angel on this earth. Working for her was my dream job. Chris's sudden appearance was definitely going to throw a wrench in my plans.

"Hi, there," he said as he crouched down and met Katie's gaze.

Out of self-preservation, I turned and pulled Katie away from him, hiding her behind my voluminous skirt. He couldn't see her blonde curls or the widow's peak that proved it'd taken two sets of DNA to make her. He couldn't discover the secret I'd been hiding all these years.

Finding my strength, I held Katie close and sidestepped Chris. "I've gotta go," I murmured as I focused on the door and made a beeline for it.

I heard him call out a farewell, but I didn't let it stop me.

I needed to get out of here before I said something stupid. Before I allowed Chris to charm me once more and I was left to deal with the consequences of our love on my own while he ran off to chase his dream.

There was one secret he could never know. It was the one secret I'd been doing a pretty good job at hiding from everyone.

If I wanted to keep my tiny family intact, he could never discover the truth.

Katie was his.

———

R eturn to the McKnight family series where the one person Penny never wanted to come back has just walked back into her life.

Reserve your copy on Amazon, today!

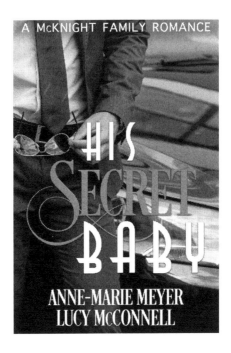

ABOUT THE AUTHOR

ANNE-MARIE MEYER

Anne-Marie Meyer lives south of the Twin Cities in MN. She spends her days with her knight in shining armor, four princes, and a baby princess.

When she's not running after her kids, she's dreaming up romantic stories. She loves to take her favorite moments in the books and movies she loves and tries to figure out a way to make them new and fresh.

Join her newsletter at anne-mariemeyer.com

ABOUT THE AUTHOR

LUCY MCCONNELL

Lucy McConnell loves romance. She is the author of the Billionaire Marriage Broker Anthology, the Marrying Miss Kringle series, and many more sweet romances.

Her short fiction has been published in *Women's World Magazine,* and she has written for *Parents' Magazine* and *The Deseret News.*

Besides fiction, Lucy also writes cookbooks. You can find her award-winning recipes under Christina Dymock.

When she's not writing, you can find Lucy volunteering at the elementary school or church, shuttling kids to basketball or rodeos, skiing with her family or curled up with a good book.
You can sign up for her newsletter—and get a **free book**—by going to https://mybookcave.com/d/290d4f96/

You can find more of her romances on Amazon.

authorlucymcconnell.wordpress.com

f

Printed in Great Britain
by Amazon

27236689R00103